IT CAME FROM SPACE III

THE NEXT GENERATION

EDDIE GENEROUS

SEVERED PRESS

IT CAME FROM SPACE III

WWW.SEVEREDPRESS.COM

ISBN: 978-1-922551-30-6

1

Lin Hubbard had to sit on the canvas Samsonite bag to get the zipper to cooperate. She'd be gone at least two weeks, most likely closer to a month. She hadn't been on assignment in nearly two years. She'd had her third child and spent much of her pregnancy and then seven months afterward doing some video interviews and not a lot else. Not that she'd really wanted to do much anyway. The new baby—while it baked in her womb, and for months afterward—was all-encompassing. Each of her children had been that way, and yet it always felt brand-new and as if she was experiencing the miracle of motherhood for the first time. At least for her. Her husband, Devon, always managed to keep the love even and spread around. This kept Trina and Conrad from pouting for attention more than they did already.

Trina was four and Conrad was five. The new baby was named June.

Lin had cried often over the last two weeks. She'd sent an email to her boss at CBC, ready to put her hat back in the task ring, and to her great surprise and sudden, terrified dismay, her boss called her cellphone after only minutes had passed. She'd assumed she'd have skads of time before he pitched a story to her.

"We need the thing on Picture Island covered.

Let's say eight parts. There's nobody else available. I've been fighting with myself over calling you, but now you've contacted me and we're not going to be late on this one. It won't be just another cold case by the time we air it," Morena Redding said from her office in Vancouver.

"Oh, yeah, sure." Lin swallowed something huge and invisible and spiky. "Maybe I can do some of the interviews over the phone or Zoom…I can't go for at least a week."

"That's fine. That's perfect. I've got student interns that can take laptops to the people in the hospital. They sent them into Vancouver General because Picture Island doesn't have any facilities… You're really saving our butts here. We need something enticing," Morena said.

What she didn't say was something enticing to attract advertisers, and thusly ensure her position, despite falling revenues since the first quarter she'd been in charge—they'd been falling before that, but the point of promoting fresh blood was to fix listenership issues.

Over the next few days, Lin had done seven interviews via Zoom with luckless survivors who were doped to the gills and one young man who was hanging around the hospital because his caretaker had been mauled. It came out quickly that he was a bit of a hero—he'd been dethroned after it turned out the beast survived the close and personal shot and then had to be blown to bits by a couple local men. George McNaughton had been by far the most interesting of all the subjects, and yet the least talkative. She had to coax and massage every response, but that was good. Perhaps not for the show, but it got her head in the game. It shook off some rust. And in the end, she got the story of how he'd shot the gator and how everyone assumed it was dead, and then how he and a girl named Jacy Popper had discovered it was alive and feeding.

She'd felt confident and ready after that, and then she started acknowledging leaving her new baby at home. It was like slowly tugging away the world's biggest and stickiest bandage.

"Giant space gator," Lin said from atop her luggage, trying not to cry.

A door opened, bringing with it a vacuum effect that rattled the picture frames on the shelves in the living room. Lin wiped her eyes before hopping down off the bag. Little feet pounded her way. First came Conrad, then came Trina.

"I got Woody!" Conrad said.

"I got Nemo!" Trina said.

Each held up a Happy Meal toy. The ads had been airing on the cartoon stations and on YouTube between videos: McDonald's was in cahoots with Disney, doing a 50th anniversary promotion and had brought out all the big guns for the toy lineup. Devon wasn't far behind, lugging the roly-poly June in his arms. She was awake and seemingly content.

"Mom, look!" Conrad said, waving the toy in his mother's face.

"I see, honey. Why don't you go play in the living room and I'll be out in a bit?" Lin said.

Conrad made a zooming plane noise that vibrated his lips and ran out of the room. Trina tried to make the noise too but could only manage to blow a raspberry as she steered the plastic fish like it was flying.

Lin pulled the luggage from the bed and sat. She lifted her arms for June. Devon passed her off without word and then sat on the bed himself.

"You're going to be okay," he said.

"I know," Lin said. She lay down, putting the baby next to her face. "You going to be a good girl?" The words came out rimmed with emotion and Lin snuffled back fresh tears.

Devon rubbed her shoulder. "You're going to do great."

"I know."

"The space gator is a pretty wild story."

"I can hardly believe it."

"The time will fly. You'll get out of the house. The real world is out there," Devon said. "You'll do great."

Lin tickled June's belly and the fat baby face scrunched up in a fit of laughter. It seemed impossible at that moment that she'd be leaving this baby ever, impossible that they couldn't be sealed in a time capsule and exist in the moment's perfection.

"I don't mean to…it's almost three. You have that meeting and then the ferry…don't you think maybe you'd best get moving?" Devon said.

Lin ignored him, cooing baby sounds as she tickled the bulbous tummy beneath the soft, soft onesie. She had to catch two ferries to get from her home to Picture Island. The first would be that evening and the next would be the following morning. The baby continued laughing, her cheeks going a merry pink.

"You have to say goodbye to Conrad and Trina, too."

Lin continued tickling. The baby's arms and legs absently motorboated in glee.

"Lin."

June scrunched her face. The stench was instant and full-bodied. Lin quit tickling.

She smiled at Devon. "Oh, look at the time."

Devon laughed as he shook his head gently. "You would," he said.

Lin wheeled her luggage out of the bedroom and toward the living room, Devon close behind her, holding June out before him at maximum distance.

2

Miriam Weever sat at one of the tables in the newly refurbished—though unfinished—dining area at the Picture House Lodge. She had an empty plate before her and a coffee cup in her hand. Her pink lipstick was stark against the porcelain rim.

"Looks different from last time I was here," she said.

Mandy Ng, owner, operator, and more recently, space gator hunter, looked around at all the fresh wood still needing to be stained and then to the bare cement floor that still needed carpet laying. "That damned gator tore it to hell in here. Had a crew working on it, but they were in the middle of something else, but came in here to get it functional for me. A favor, sort of."

"Oh, interesting…I mean, that was quite a thing I guess?" Miriam said. She was from the mainland and worked for ReMax as a realtor. She'd come to take snapshots and to gather information on more than twenty properties suddenly needing listed.

"It was a thing all right. Refill?" Mandy lifted the coffee pot higher.

"Oh, why not?" Miriam said.

"So how many houses are going up?"

Miriam eyed the coffee flowing into the mug. "Total, must be twenty-five. I don't have all the listings. I saw a couple go up privately and then Gerard Bates from Century21 has some done remotely. You should see the pictures." She rolled her eyes and made a gagging face. "Gerard didn't want to make the trip and it'll be my gain. It takes a little knowhow to make some places look saleable and the pics the sellers sent him are plain…well, bad."

"I see," Mandy said.

The breakfast crowd had gone off and the lunch crowd had yet to file in. That left only Mandy, Miriam, and in the kitchen washing dishes was the young motormouth, Jacy Popper. The cruise her parents were on was stuck down near Seattle. Everyone was sick onboard and had to stay put until it was all figured out. Jacy's uncle had gone to see Mandy after two weeks of minding the girl to beg Mandy to offer her a job. Mandy had gotten to know Jacy some the night when the shit really hit the fan. They worked out an under the table deal. She knew Jacy would be slower than anyone she'd hired before, and she knew the girl would yap her head off whenever Mandy was in the kitchen with her, but she also knew she didn't want to do all the dishes herself. She was lately feeling too old to wash strangers' dishes more than a few hours a day. So Jacy had the job: $5 an hour, from 11:30 AM to 6:30 PM, $35 every night when she left, cash on the nail. Plus, all the fries she could eat.

"I have a hot buyer, I'm thinking he'll invest in a good many, and if that doesn't work, I'm going to guess there'll be a revolving door here for a while. All the attention will have city people looking at the listing and mooning over simplicity. They'll move out here, stay six months and run back when they get bored," Miriam said.

"As long as they come for breakfast while they're here," Mandy said, half-joking. She didn't much care for out-of-towners who came in oozing condescension, saying things like 'It's so quaint,' then asking for the origin story behind the eggs on the menu, and then grimacing when Mandy always responded, 'Eggs come from chicken's asses.'

3

"Ah, to hell with yas," Gerd Hamilton said as he stumbled out of his one-room home about a mile north of town and a half-mile from where the national park lands began. The afternoon was quickly becoming evening, the sun was still out but its force had significantly dwindled. Gerd had polished off close to a liter of wickedly potent dandelion wine—he made it himself in huge casks. He sold two casks a year and sat on another two for personal consumption. Other times of the year he ran lines on maple trees for syrup. He sold most of that, though saved several liters to mix in with the corn whiskey he distilled. The rest of the corn he ate or fed to chickens. Though his home was small, his property was big enough to offer self-sustainability. Something his wife and daughter had been all for, at first.

They'd left him more than twelve years ago and since then, he'd cursed their memory every day. Usually after partaking in a goodly sum of one of his homebrews.

Not everything he consumed came from his land. He poached mushrooms, small game, and the maple sap from the national forest. If the rangers knew he was doing it, they never said. He also cleared away deadfall to turn into firewood, which was the goal of today's drunken journey. He climbed into a 1981, manure brown, F-150.

The seats were cracked and revealed the bright yellow foam that would've otherwise been hidden. The dash was crooked and thick with years upon years of dust. The windshield was a series of spiderwebs. The belts whined like banshees upon first engaging the engine. Otherwise, the truck was the only really good, reliable thing in Gerd's life these days.

Driving drunk was no problem. He had only a few miles to go to a recently bountiful locale, and he'd been behind the wheel while intoxicated so often his equilibrium had reached sloppy perfection—driving sober, he might've been more of a worry. Slow and steady, he hooked off the highway down an ancient logging road. The national park lands were so big, it would've been simply bad luck to run into one of the rangers, and then double that bad luck for that ranger to say something. The way Gerd saw it, he wasn't part of the island's population, he was an animal fixture. He was a growly bear that people would be wise to avoid.

"*I can't get no…,*" he sang along. Cassette one of a two-part greatest hits album had been lodged in his stereo deck for close to twenty years. The sound was getting crackly and, in some spots, made piercing electronic glitch noises. None of that mattered. He never rode longer than ten, maybe fifteen minutes. "*…I try, and I try, and.*"

Gerd killed the engine and kicked open his door. He sat a moment amid the buzzing in his head and the buzzing from the door's sensor. The road had washed away in some areas, though the forest floor was only a couple feet lower.

He followed one of these muddy dips, picking up unattainable speed for a moment before reaching a perfect tree to stumble against. The birch bark was hard and unforgiving, and yet had no lower limbs or jagged accents to cause him any discomforts once sober in the early morning. He was rough, and he was addicted, and he was unlikeable, but he didn't drink before noon. Once stopped, he immediately turned back toward the truck. He couldn't cut much wood without a chainsaw.

He got the tailgate down, swaying as if at sea. He checked for gasoline and then the oil. Both appeared fine. He wiped syrupy red oil from the cap on his filthy pantleg before hoisting the battered Stihl chainsaw free. He took the decline into the forest a little slower this time. Not five feet away was a suitable log. It had been thunderstruck.

"*I try, and I try, and I try,*" he mumble-sang as he centered the lefthand chainsaw grip at the fork of his crotch. He pulled the recoil handle six quick jerks before the engine lit. He quickly grabbed the trigger and gave it some juice. The chain spun and the engine whined.

Gerd stumbled over to the felled log and eyed out a stove length—he'd have to chop the wood later to fit into his stove, but that was a morning task. The chain bit into the log, sending out a shower of sawdust. He then pitched forward, the chainsaw finding air instead of wood. It was nothing but a shell in the middle.

He squinted as he pulled the log apart, the Stihl engine rumbling along unacknowledged. It looked a bit like the work of ants, but he'd never seen such a thorough job done of it. Something moved within the shadows. Gerd reefed back the end chunk. The chainsaw began sputtering.

"Jesus!" he said, rolling sideways as he reached for the chainsaw's handles.

From the hole came an ant the size of a poodle. It made a high wincey sound before charging at Gerd, its antennae dancing, its mandibles pinching opened and closed, its nightmare eyes glued to its target.

Gerd yanked up the Stihl and the engine buzzed while the chain sawed into the creature's head. Amber fluid sprayed free as the ant's head was chewed by the chain's teeth, reeling in its boney structure. The skull was tough enough to stop the chain and stall the engine. Gerd took several deep breaths where he lay, knowing he had to have imagined it.

"Got enough wood for today anyway," he said and pushed to his knees, looking away from the ant. He climbed to his feet and stumbled in the direction of the truck.

"*Reeet ree ruh, reeet ree ruh!*"

The sound was incredibly loud. Like a squeaky chair swing next to a microphone. Like an obscenely large treefrog. Just as the thought connected, so too did a great wet slap. It wasn't a hand and Gerd had no way of knowing what it was. It had covered his forehead, eyes, and nose, and it hadn't retracted in the way a palm did.

Instead, it retracted with him in tow, lashing him through the air, high into the trees above. At the last moment, the hold slipped a hair and he saw the suctioning cups and the telltale ridges of a pink, pink tongue. He also saw the cavernous mouth of a frog big enough to bite off his head and shoulders. Everything went black and reeked of swamp and fish.

He began bouncing as the frog attempted to swallow him. His arms flailed as he wrenched around, trying to pull himself free. His face began to burn in the acid of the frog's guts. He inhaled deeply. Fluid popped into his throat and gushed into his lungs. He tried to scream again, kicking and swinging uselessly as he was deteriorated from the inside and outside by the frog's digestive fluids.

The world tilted and Gerd spun free, starfishing through the air on his way to the forest floor. He was blind, each inhalation was torture, and the flesh of his face had formed a rind of rusty crust from the burns of that short-lived battle. He pushed to his feet and stumbled blindly, only able to withstand the agony thanks to the dandelion wine he'd drunk. He was moving deeper into the forest, trying to run and shout, accomplishing neither.

The floor beneath him tilted and he picked up speed, barely keeping afoot, until nailing a soft, greasy wall. He dropped backward and, terrified the frog was behind him, got to his knees and crawled. His face struck a soft wall and its prickly bristles. He connected dots and concluded he'd come against a barrier of felled pine trees.

The incredible, honking roar that rattled him deep into his guts had him second-guessing this conclusion. The wall moved and Gerd lost his equilibrium again. He lay flat, his burnt crispy face, useless eyes, and voiceless mouth pointed at the foot-wide hoof a second before it stamped down and destroyed his head.

4

Denver Jones, the astronomer who'd first come in search of a meteorite, had extended his vacation. His coworkers and boss were all for his leave, given the incredible nature of what had happened on the island since he'd been there, and that he'd become a smalltime international celebrity on news stations. Jerome Hawkins, a physicist who'd been cornered into coming and had stayed thanks to intrigue, was also quite pleased with Denver Jones' choice to stick around Picture Island a little longer. The locals, however, weren't so enthusiastic.

Denver had made it all too clear in the heat of the moment that he thought sacrificing some local life would be a reasonable trade for catching the gator-like creature alive. In the end, the creature was blown to bits and Denver had a good number of specimens sent off to two different labs for examination.

"I'm heading back tomorrow," Jerome said as they walked along the pier.

They had taken a large, early supper and both were quietly releasing gases amid the noise and fresh air of the seaside. Denver nodded to the comment. He'd have to get back sooner than later, but something held him steadfast to the little town separated from its next closest neighbor by seventy miles of ocean. Though he hadn't said it, the complete destruction of the creature didn't feel like the end, or at least hadn't felt like a *suitable* end. There was something about it, like a revenant slasher about to rise from his grave and begin swinging a machete anew.

The scene had been good for the few local businesses that existed and had been an outright boon to whoever owned the ferry system, and somehow that gave room for more. People came in droves, a few brought along food carts and sold hot dogs and tacos and shawarma without licenses. Some locals posted hand-painted B&B signs in the windows of their modest homes. Four young women were running a daily tour group of all the spots in town the creature had destroyed. Once a week the group did an extended tour and rode in matching 1994 Ford Windstar vans up to the hot springs, where they got out and wandered everywhere that wasn't green, as if they were afraid to touch the forest. Denver and Jerome had taken the tour once themselves, and Denver pointed out all the times that the guide fibbed or exaggerated, though did so under his breath and for his friend's ear only.

"Are you sticking around a while longer?" Jerome said.

Denver slowed a step so he was downwind when he let loose a hot little fart that suggested sooner than later he needed to make his way to a toilet. "I suppose so. I don't think I could get much real work done until I hear back about the specimens. The genetic and elemental makeup of the creature is yet quite a mystery."

Jerome sighed. “I hate to admit it, but all signs point to space. I was so certain that it couldn’t be true, I’ve been willfully blind.”

“Nothing *is* until it is proven.”

“Yes, but to simplify: if *it* isn’t from here, it’s from someplace else.”

Denver knew without a doubt the gator-like creature’s egg had come from space. He also knew Jerome refused that likelihood whenever it was presented to him. He’d only accept it as fact in the quiet space of mutual respect, friendship, and the notion of original conclusion. Denver imagined one of Jerome’s co-workers suggesting that if searched in the dictionary, the antonym for teamwork would read *Jerome Hawkins*. He imagined the scene like it was a TV sitcom and they’d have to double the laugh track for that particular quip.

“What will change for you, once you know for certain the elements are not of Earth?” Jerome said.

“I don’t know,” Denver said. “I suppose the question being exhausted to its current extreme will have to do. The suggestion of any life elsewhere also opens space for intelligent life elsewhere.”

“The current being our historical current,” Jerome said, not a question.

The pair leaned on the railing of the pier, looking out at the gentle waves as they roiled into and over themselves. They probably wouldn’t have much reason to keep in touch beyond social media, and in the current—a much more immediate current in the historical sense—both were feeling melancholy about the idea. Friendships in adulthood weren't so easy to come by.

5

Jacy Popper was sweaty, wet, and stinking of fryer grease. She'd just collected her cash from Mandy for the day's work. She guessed Mandy paid her daily on the assumption that one day Jacy wouldn't show up for her shift and both of them would be okay with it. What Mandy didn't know was that Jacy was lonely; her aunt, uncle, and cousins had come to dislike her, and she wanted her parents. At least if she kept busy working, she couldn't annoy anyone with her mouth, which, no matter how hard she tried, she couldn't shut it for very long.

Instead of going straight home, she detoured to Space Gator Entertainment to look at the comic books Lucy Weight had in stock. The flimsy books on the shelves hadn't changed in the last two weeks, but she perused like they were new and she might find a golden nugget. Every day after work, she bought a Fun Dip packet and one of the horror comics.

She read the horror comics because she wanted an excuse to Zoom call George McNaughton. He was stuck in a hotel room across the road from the hospital until his Aunt Carole was let out. With no help system awaiting her at home, Carole had to stay put until she could complete most of the activities of daily living on her own, but she'd contracted an infection and was now so ill she hardly recognized the children supposedly under her care.

Every evening over Zoom, Jacy would read George her new comic and he would read one a man also stuck in the hospital had picked up for him—the man's wife was sick with the kind of thing that had no way back. The man bought him a whole box worth after George sat emptyhanded in a waiting room, surrounded by magazines.

"Nothing worth reading?" the man had said.

George only shrugged.

The man nodded. "What are you, nine or ten? When I was your age, there was this old guy. I mowed his lawn and one time he paid me to help clean out his basement. He had just about every EC and Black Cat and Weird comic there was. All pre-code, that was before—"

"Like *Tales from the Crypt?*" George said, suddenly engaged.

The man grinned. "Now what do you know about pre-code horror?"

"The Golden Age…but Silver and Bronze are good too. My friend Jacy even has some good new ones."

The man shook his head gently, gazing off into space.

The next day he showed up with a big stack of cheap Bronze Age horror comics and a copy of a huge book titled *The Horror! The Horror!* The book had dozens of pre-code comics printed within, as well as a wealth of history on the topic.

"Is there something I should order in?" Lucy said to Jacy. When the store was open, she was there. There was no employee beneath owner/manager, at least not yet.

There were three other patrons in the store, two of whom milled around the little room with the beaded curtain and a placard reading MUST BE 18 OR OLDER TO ENTER but seemed too nervous to step through the door.

"George likes the Golden Age, but I think that is too much money. They're collectable. People collect them. Like art. They got banned. George was telling me all about it. He says everyone agreed to sell only comics approved by the comic authority and the comic authority banned everything fun. Couldn't even have crime or horror or terror in the title," Jacy said.

"So, is that a no?" Lucy said.

"I'll just get these ones," Jacy said, holding up the first two issues of *Soul Plumber*.

Lacy looked at the comics and then to Jacy, her face scrunched sideways. "Uh, think those are mature."

"More mature than blowing up a space gator?" Jacy said. "I think I should be able to get whatever because I worked for the money, and I was there when—"

"I know! Got it! You told me. Twelve even, after tax," Lucy said.

Jacy handed over the cash and accepted the comics back from Lucy. She hurried away then, passing the night tour group and their guide who regularly lied about being present during the gator attack. Jacy wanted to call the guide out, but wanted to get home more, and wanted to hop on her tablet and call George the most.

6

Vicki Taylor and Jeff Randolph snuck away from the rest of the tour group and headed up the hill in Vicki's Audi e-tron. Picture Island had been a lot less exciting than what they'd hoped for; they blamed the tour guides and the seemingly endless construction going on. The town should've been preserved in a semi-demolished state, really keeping the moment alive for tourists and their tourist money. But no.

The next best thing was going up the hill to see the destroyed house and take a dip in the hot springs where the gator had ambushed a construction crew and an artist. Nature had taken care of the blood and traffic had taken care of most of the good prints. Though for some reason, people were reverential about stomping around the forest much. Vicki and Jeff had plans of making the space their own. Why let perfectly good social content go to waste just because some hicks were eaten by a giant lizard?

They rolled up the dark, dark path. Jeff rode shotgun. He withdrew a pre-rolled joint from a pack and lit it with a disposable Cricket lighter. He inhaled deeply and immediately barked out a cough. Vicki chuckled and held out her hand, index and middle finger spread, creating a perfect parking space for the joint.

"Just a second. I'll put together a TikTok." Jeff held his phone up and took a deep drag from the joint and blew it onto the screen. He panned slowly to Vicki. "Space Gator tour," he said and then tapped the stop button. He'd conglomerate a dozen or so small clips into about three perfect minutes.

Vicki put up her hand again and this time, Jeff transferred the joint to her. She took a drag and held it. It was only a couple minutes more before they reached the widened piece of road that acted as the hot springs parking lot.

"I have an idea," Vicki said. "We get out and you shoot from right at the hood and walk backwards, passing me until you get my whole silhouette. Then I strip."

TikTok had rules about content, so one had to be crafty not to get banned while also arousing viewers. Vicki had had two accounts banned in the past. She'd had a handful of cosmetic surgeries over the last couple years and it seemed almost a crime not to share the body Dr. Shinnamin had sculpted for her.

"Perfect," Jeff said.

He'd had nearly as many procedures, though most of his involved hair removal. The only truly invasive surgery was a penile elongation procedure he'd had in Brazil that provided him an additional inch thanks to a molded and sutured hunk of rib cartilage.

He stood in front of the Audi with his cellphone poised to shoot the darkness. The headlights were on and would flare nicely in the video once he began backing up.

"Ready," he said and glanced over his shoulder. She was slightly to his right and he'd veer left as he reversed. This would be sweet, sweet content.

"Go ahead," Vicki said. She was in a hoodie and jeans, barefoot—she'd already slipped out of her leather boots.

"Three-two…" Jeff trailed.

He hit record and started walking backward slowly. Vicki gave him a sexy pout, which he wasn't sure the camera picked up, and continued by until she was a dark shape amid the blue headlight shine. He pointed a finger gun, and she began to strip, spreading her legs and bending toward the camera once the jeans passed her hips and butt. She wore no underwear. Her feet got to the tedious task of kicking away the jeans while she turned slightly to offer a curved silhouette as her hoodie rose. She tossed it onto the hood of the Audi. She peeled off her bra next, then held it before one of the headlights, the lace clear and tantalizing. She tossed the bra with her sweater and stepped slowly off camera.

"Perfect," Jeff said.

He would've liked to do a silhouette shot as well. Thanks to the surgery, he was a show-er who liked to pretend he was also a grower, but where TikTok was stern with the female body, it was downright prudish when it came to the man's body, or at least when it came to dongs.

Vicki had gone around to the hatchback for

drinks while Jeff got to stripping without an audience in mind. Vicki hopped behind the wheel of the Audi and rolled in reverse, repositioning the headlights at three steamy pools. The sulfur smell was heavy and strangely inviting.

"Have to make sure your nipples stay below the water," Jeff said.

This was easier said than done. As Cardi B had said, '*If it's up, then it's stuck,*' and with silicone implants, her breasts became almost like floatation devices.

They got into the first pool, offering thoughtless *ahhs* at the lovely heat and bubbles. Jeff swigged from his beer before moving to set it aside. He reached out of the pool to put it on the ground and grabbed his joint pack. He lit a pre-roll and handed it off to Vicki. The bubbles were being helpful, muddying up the surf to the point where areolas became inconclusive to the viewfinder.

"Take a sexy puff and exhale slowly. Ready?"

Vicki nodded.

"Three, two…"

She inhaled deeply and blew out the smoke. It danced through the Audi's headlights like summer dust motes past a window. She tapped the ash absently before tipping a green Beck's bottle to her pouty, collagen-filled lips. Jeff turned the camera back toward him.

He waggled his eyebrows. "Think she'll let me play which hole feels the best?"

"I know which hole," Vicki said and gave a gentle splash.

Jeff spun the camera and Vicki was turned away, rising slow, slow, slow from the water until her entire ass was out. He'd have to clip the last second or so, but this video would be good for a few hundred likes for sure.

"The weed's getting to me, so you better not have been joking," Vicki said, her ass still up above the water.

Jeff said nothing. Instead, he stood and stepped carefully along the slim rock lining the inside of the pool. There were levels beneath their feet, though the escaping heat made poor footing more forgiving than in a regular pool. They grunted, groaned, splashed, and moaned. The act lasted six satisfying minutes—they'd been together four years and had all the right moves worked out with countless hours of practice.

Once done, Vicki luxuriated in the pool. Jeff was next to her, editing the video clips within the TikTok app. He watched through his cuts twice, pausing at a moment between turning the camera from Vicki to himself. A pair of bulbous black shapes reflected light a bit overhead and behind them in the image on the screen.

"Post it yet?" Vicki said.

Jeff forgot about the shapes and pulled the trigger on the post. "Here's hoping we don't get my account banned."

"No nudity, should be okay." She didn't sound all that confident.

Jeff opened his flashlight app and tapped it to life. He shined into the blackness beyond where the headlights reached. He tilted the shine higher into the trees and saw nothing untoward. It was just forest; could've been anything out there or it could've been the weed.

"What? A bat or something?" Vicki said.

"No…I thought I saw something. It was bigger than a bat. A lot bigger."

The forest sounds began to pick up when the human sounds quieted. Distantly, large animals called to each other, sending great echoes up the hillside and through the trees. Having an echo bypass all the elements between seemed unlikely, almost impossible, and yet, it had happened.

Jeff was about to dose the camera flash and check on the early returns of the video he'd posted when something big and shadowy moved high in the trees.

"What was that?" Vicki said.

Jeff tilted the cellphone higher but didn't need to. From the deep shadows, a spider dropped on a thread as thick as clothesline. The spider itself was the size of a beanbag chair. Its huge black eyes had been what Jeff caught on camera.

Vicki burst from the pool and the spider lashed out, nailing into her back with a venomous secretion that left her paralyzed. Jeff hadn't moved. The spider seemed to watch him even as Vicki's prone form slid deeper into the water. A moment before its furry feet got wet, it leapt onto Jeff's face. He screamed. Matching needle-like fixtures within the spider's mandible lashed out and instantly sent him into a fog. He slipped and floated on his back, unable to act even as the spider used its thick web to reel them one at a time from the water and wrap them in individual silky sacks. They were then pulled high into the trees where they were just two of almost a dozen feed sacks being saved for later.

7

George was in the hotel room with his sister, Alexis, and the cat they'd inherited named Bozo. Alexis was sleeping on her stomach while the cat was perched on the windowsill, looking out at the busy Thursday night. George was in the bathtub with Carole's laptop so he wouldn't keep Alexis awake while he Zoom chatted with Jacy. When Alexis didn't get a good ten to twelve hours of sleep, she became a real crank. Things were trying enough without her being upset.

Into the camera, George had read a story from an issue of Unexpected about a wishing well with grave consequences, playing show and tell with the panels as he went. Jacy had read the first issue of *Soul Plumber*. It wasn't as fun, but the story was much bigger and nastier, which George liked, though he doubted it was meant for an eleven-year-old and a thirteen-year-old. Comics, and regular books and movies like that always had stuff that went over his head.

"How's the hotel? I've stayed in lots of hotels," Jacy said, stopping herself. She'd told George all about every hotel she'd been in already, a couple of the stories she had probably told him twice by now.

"I won't be here too long. Carole's friend is

coming for us and we're going down to California with her until Carole is better," George said, solemnly.

"Oh no. You'll be way far away. But maybe you can go see the Hollywood sign and take selfies with famous people. I want to go to Hollywood someday. My dad calls it Hollyweird. He thinks he's funny. He stole it from some director who was doing an interview, and *that* guy called Hollywood Hollyweird."

George hadn't considered that he'd be further away, as it seemed the same distance through Zoom, but maybe it wasn't.

"Do you even know this woman? What if she's mean and stinks and has a fruit cellar full of rotten jars like my great-grandmother had after she died, and we had to help clean out her house so it could go up for sale?"

George had considered a good many things worse than funky jars and bad odors. He was feeling tugged around and hopeless. Nothing was his fault and yet it all felt like it was his fault; everything going to hell carried a burden of guilt.

"Too bad you can't come back here. There's all kinds of houses for sale. You could stay in one and I could sneak out. I make thirty-five bucks a day. That's enough for groceries and I get all the free fries. I could bring some for you. Soggy fries aren't great, but they're better than nothing," Jacy said.

George stared across the small washroom. Carole's purse was there with her stuff. She'd told George the pin on her debit card before the infection settled in and she always had to be doped up or sleeping. He could take out cash, get a cab to the ferry terminal, and walk on like anybody else. Alexis and Bozo could go with Carole's friend.

"I think I will do that?" he said.

"Do what?"

"Come there and stay in an empty house."

"No way!" Jacy said.

"Yes, way," George said. "Hardly anyone will even notice."

"Are you bringing your sister?"

George shook his head. "She's too little."

Over the next few minutes, George and Jacy worked out a plan. He'd swipe the debit card, take a cab, and ride the ferry—Jacy said that was perfect. She'd scope out a couple houses where he could squat. Neither considered the long-term notion of the plan, all that mattered was the here and now. And, though it wouldn't be said aloud, their getting back together. The kissing they'd done before he shipped off felt more and more like true love every day they were apart, every day they were surrounded by people and still feeling utterly alone.

8

Mandy got up early enough to take a walk before she had to take any breakfast orders. She carried her long rifle, resting its barrel against her shoulder. It seemed to dwarf her, though whenever the need called for her to fire it, she had no trouble doing so. Her not firing it in quite some time was part of the reason she'd gone for a walk up the trail next to the road—if she stayed on it long enough, several hours, it would meander up to the hot springs. Routinely, usually multiple times a day, she'd had to scare a grizzly out of her dumpster. Since the thing with the gator, she hadn't seen any bears, or deer, or moose. The hope was that they were in hiding or simply sticking to the wilds and hadn't become chow for a ravenous creature.

"Ooh, look at you," she said and bent at the knees, setting the rifle down at her feet.

She plucked nine pine mushrooms from the base of a dead pine tree that had been standing in that place more than double the years she'd been alive—so, safely into triple digits. The mushrooms went into the deep pockets of her flannel jacket. Before rising, she scanned the immediate vicinity for more mushrooms and found a massive slug, one ten times as big as she'd ever seen before. Its head bulged out in hideous Elephant Man lumps and its optical tentacles appeared to be leaning forward like limp noodles, as if deflated. The scales on its back were littered with open sores that oozed the gushy brown fluid that worked like blood, delivering nutrients throughout the slug's body.

A discarded Walmart bag had come to rest at the base of another tree. Mandy decided she'd best show this dead critter to someone. She made a mitt of the wet bag and grabbed the slug. It was surprisingly weighty.

"Uck! You nasty…" she trailed.

She dropped the slug upon seeing what was beneath it. Writhing in a pale grey mass were larva of some kind. Each was as big as a pen lid. She thought a moment and came to a better conclusion. She dug around her jacket pockets and found a fuzzy plastic poppy from last November's Remembrance Day. She felt a little guilty about it but set the phony red flower down next to the flipped slug, using it to present scale. She withdrew her phone and took a picture.

She pocketed the phone and picked up her rifle. She shot a glance back at the slug and cringed as she began stepping deeper into the woods. Over the years, she'd tromped on dozens of banana slugs and black slugs, she thought if she stepped on one that big, it might take her foot off. She shivered, her gaze playing out to the forest and to the furry white breast of a deer. Her eyes traveled up and up. What should've been a deer that maxed out at about six feet, was a deer that stood closer to twelve.

Smoothly as possible, she withdrew her phone again. She opened the camera app and clicked a shot. The deer burst off at about the same moment, or a moment after, so she hoped. She checked the shot. It was nothing but a brown and white blur amidst the dense greens and greys of the woods.

“Something is not right,” she said.

She’d taken to running enough times on the island, but this time felt different. Somehow, the threat felt bigger than a curious grizzly bear with a taste for kitchen garbage. This felt even bigger than a space gator with a taste for human flesh.

9

Lin got off a video call with Devon and the kids a minute or so after the boarding announcement rang out through the packed lot. She was so stressed she stopped on the way to grab a pack of Du Marrier cigarettes. To her surprise, they'd removed the typical branding and flavor labeling. All that was left was a great big warning sign and the brand title in smallish lettering. She'd also purchased a fun little torch lighter—she decided it was fun because she paid $9 for it as they were all out of anything else besides barbeque lighters. At least the torch fit in her pocket and gave her room to imagine scenarios, mostly burning damp things while camping.

She hadn't smoked in ten years—well, maybe a few here and there: New Year's Eve, Christmas, her best friend Lori's bachelorette party—but this seemed like a reasonable time to indulge herself. It's not as if she was going to take up the habit again. Not at those prices.

She'd gotten to the terminal just in time for the woman at the window to say she'd be one of the last cars on for that sailing. So many people were going to Picture Island, and what she knew of the place made it totally improbable. There was only one hotel—her room was reserved—and she hoped like hell they weren't the kind of establishment that overbooked.

She followed an ancient Land Rover onboard. Rolling over the drawbridge clanged and pinged in heavy steel cries. She hit the brake when the attendant minding her row gave her a stop hand. She killed the engine and gathered herself. She needed more coffee. She needed a snack. She needed to pee. She needed…to be at home with June. She took a deep breath and exhaled slowly. She'd do this one series and then be back to family duty for the foreseeable future.

Since it was all over and totally fresh, she could probably get all the interview fodder she needed in a few days. If she recorded at night, she could find a local to take her around to all the important spots during the day. She could select the best sound bites and put together the narrative when she should be sleeping. Hell, she might get home by Sunday.

She yawned.

Pipe dreams. She needed to sleep. She needed to do a good job if she wanted good opportunities in the future.

"Suck it up," she whispered.

She followed a line of passengers up the steep, steep stairs from the parking levels. The air was thick with seawater and car exhaust. Once to the top, she followed her nose and found the cafeteria-style restaurant. She grabbed a vacuum-sealed Danish and a large cup of coffee. The coffee was good, full-bodied without any acidity. The Danish tasted like icing sugar and lemons pasted atop the kind of cake that's uniquely available in situations where better options are simply too inconvenient—gas stations, snack machines, on BC Ferries.

She grabbed a free paper—she couldn't really work until she had a better idea of the whole of the story—and sat on one of the padded seats. Two rows away, she spotted George McNaughton. She recognized him from their Zoom conversation.

"What are you up to?" she said to herself.

She knew his caretaker was in the hospital, and he'd suggested the expectation was that she'd be there for another couple weeks, at least. She slipped the paper under her arm and took her coffee and what remained of the Danish, and stepped through the rows of seats over to where George sat. He was like an island in a sea of empty spaces.

"George? Mind if I sit?" she said.

He gasped, his eyes wide, as if he'd been caught.

Lin didn't wait and sat. "You want some Danish? It's too sweet for me."

George shook his head gently.

The buzz of humanity filled in around them, and rather than making them a piece of the larger puzzle, it further intensified their apartness. Everyone was happy or excited. Some people had to be locals because they amalgamated into small pockets of chatter. Children ran in socked feet. Teenagers huddled around handheld devices.

Three of the one hundred or so visible in that section were reading paperbacks.

"You didn't tell me you were going back. Is your...was it your aunt? Is she out of the hospital?" Lin said.

George swallowed.

Lin frowned. "Are you riding alone?"

George nodded.

Lin paused a moment, going through all the information she had on this kid. "Your grandmother—is that right? She was who you were visiting on Picture Island. She died, and she was your only family there. Do I have that correct?"

She wouldn't have been so bold and assuming of authority if George weren't a child. This despite that he'd saved his family and a man named Denver Jones from the gator, and that he'd been present at the gator's final demise.

George studied his hands rather than answering.

Lin's fast mind began piecing the bits of information together and that funny name *popped* into her head. "Jacy Popper? Is she your girlfriend?"

"Yes," George said, almost whispering it.

Lin rocked slowly, nodding with her entire upper body. "And you're going to see her?"

"I didn't want to go with Carole's friend to California...I don't even know her."

It struck Lin then that she hadn't thought about June or the rest of her family in the last five minutes. Which proved something she'd assumed to be true but somehow couldn't imagine it being so: she could put her mind on something other than her baby and focus on a mystery.

"Does nobody know you're here?"

George's lip curled and he looked around at all the strangers. "Jacy knows."

"You'll be driving your…Carole's friend crazy with worry." Lin pulled out her cellphone as if to call the hospital. There were no bars as they'd already made it far enough from shore, but her focus didn't quite get to the point of acknowledgement. She could use George. He would be the ultimate tour guide and she could get home sooner than later. "Would you be up for helping me when we reach the island?"

"Okay," George said.

"You do recognize me, right?"

George nodded.

"Good. But we also need to call the hospital to let Carole know you're going back on the first ferry out tomorrow morning," Lin said.

There were two more sailings scheduled for tonight that could take him across, but he'd be busy. The boy was a bit of nitrous boost in the middle of her race to get home.

"Why?" George said.

"Why do we have to call?"

"No, why tomorrow?"

Lin sat back and lifted her coffee cup. It hovered before her mouth. "Because I need a tour guide and an in-depth account from you and Jacy Popper." She sipped. This boy was going to have her home in no time at all.

10

Denver had sat with Jerome Hawkins for breakfast and then thought about him after he'd gone away. He was suddenly lonely. As far as he knew, he had the only extensively educated mind left on the island. The longer he stuck around, the more he'd notice it, likely.

He stepped into the dining room of the Picture House Lodge for a late lunch and Mandy buzzed over to him directly. She carried a coffee pot and a cellphone.

"Look at this thing," she said without preamble and turned the small screen of her cellphone toward Denver.

He leaned in closer, trying to understand. "What's that flower?"

"It's a Remembrance Day poppy," she said. When he still harbored an expression of confusion, she added, "It's for our version of Veterans Day. It's a little bigger than a toonie." She reached into her apron and withdrew a coin—either she'd stupidly left the poppy in the forest, or she'd dropped it along the way because she couldn't find it now. She looked at the coin in her hand. "I guess a bit bigger than that." She set the coin on the table.

Denver looked at the coin and then back to the

picture. His eyes drifted to the coin but returned like a bullet to the image. He understood that what he was looking at was a slug—he'd seen hundreds of them since he'd been on the island—but massive and covered in equally as massive larva of some sort.

"I think I'm going crazy. This wasn't all. I saw a white tail deer…it was huge," Mandy said.

Denver squinted up at her. "How huge?"

"Huge, huge. Like…more than double my height. Bigger than a moose," Mandy said. She turned her phone back and found the useless photo she'd taken of a brown and white blur.

"That's not a great picture," he said.

"I know that. I was just showing you to show that I tried to get a shot of it, too, and not only the slug. But the slug wasn't moving. I didn't know it was covered in nastier bugs until I tried to pick it up."

Denver tilted his head and pursed his lips. Impressed.

"Not with my bare hand. I used a grocery bag like a glove."

The lunch crowd had mostly cleared away. Three local men sat at a table in the corner drinking coffee. At two other tables, men in fancy leather boots and tight jeans, marine wool sweaters, sat alone with half-finished plates of food before them. They could've been brothers if they'd been the same race.

"Can you get away? Show me where you found the slug?"

Mandy looked far over her shoulder to the steel

clock on the wall. "Not really. I told a group of men about it already. They went out looking."

"Oh."

"I wanted to tell you first because you're…experienced-ish. But they were here and they missed the action on account of all being on the ball team and getting too drunk and missing the boat until the morning after everything had settled."

That made perfect sense to Denver. He'd been in the thick of it both nights and still wanted to know what came next. That explosion looked, smelled, and physically felt like a total ending, but something lingered, and maybe this was it. What if that slug was in the egg with the gator-like creature?

"An eleven-foot white tail deer?" he said.

Mandy nodded. "Coffee?"

"Yeah. And a burger and fries." He needn't specify further. He'd eaten at least ten burgers at the lodge since he'd been there. Some for lunch. Some for supper. Always with lettuce, banana peppers, onions, and ketchup. "And directions to the slug."

"Coming right up."

Mandy disappeared and Denver mused as he stirred cream and sugar into his coffee. He gazed about him. This little island was something else and changing all the time. Even the people were hugely different from when he'd arrived; what more would shift, what more would reveal itself?

11

Sergei and Ilya were the reason the foursome had missed the boat back after the ball tournament had ended. Most of the team had seemed to forget about celebrating in the face of a giant animal sighting. Sergei and Ilya wrote off the animal and began describing the bears that lived in every Russian basement instead of rats, or rather, alongside the rats.

The pair had managed to coax two young men away from the ferry to a sports bar where a boxing match was on every TV and the drinks were overpriced. Each had visited the ATM in the lobby three times before the night was through. Collectively, they had polished off the bar's two bottles of Smirnoff, a half bottle of Grey Goose, and nine pitchers of apple cider.

Tommy and Russell were the young men and coated the entire bathroom of their shared hotel room in vomit while the Russians rubbed their backs and promised they'd feel better soon. Everybody drank too much sometimes.

Once they got home—a couple days later thanks to problems with the ferry—they were crushed by the news that something much, much bigger than a Russian bear had trounced through town before being blown up. When Mandy showed them the picture she took of the slug, and explained where she'd seen it, it felt almost like a window of redemption was suddenly available.

Tommy and Russell carried shotguns while the Russians carried bolt-action rifles. They all dressed the part of off-season hunter: drab clothes, few colors, heavy boots. Sweat was running beneath arms and around collars, but the spirits remained high.

"Supposed to be around here, eh?" Tommy said.

They'd reached and passed where Mandy had found the slug and the grey critters feeding upon it. The critters had left barely a stain on the grass after finishing their feast.

"Somewhere," Ilya said. "Look at this." He pointed at a hoof print in the soft mud. It was half as long as his boot and a little bit wider.

Sergei knelt to look closer, setting his rifle by his foot as he did so. "Is big like…ovtsebyk," he said.

"Muskox," Ilya said. "There's nothing like that here?"

"Those great big furry things?" Russell said.

"No way," Tommy said.

Sergei picked up his rifle and rose. "Something big, big, big out here. Not alligator. Something else."

The four men paused, holding in their breaths. They were big and strong. In the forest they seemed less so. Everything was biggish in a forest on a Pacific Northwestern island.

"Yo," Russell whispered and pointed through

the trees directly to their collective right.

A rabbit stood just shy of four-feet-tall, its nose and jaw working endlessly. Its black eyes were empty, hollow, infinite. Rabbits didn't grow that big on Picture Island. They didn't grow a third of that big. It had them frozen, despite that they had all shot and had all eaten rabbit many times on the island. Probably Mandy would buy it from them and make a stew special for a whole week.

It was Sergei who came out of the daze first. He lifted his rifle slowly and took aim. There was so much to point at. He matched the sights with the space between and above the rabbit's eyes and pulled the trigger. The shot echoed into the woods before disappearing quickly.

The smoke exiting the rifle barrel was the only movement for one, two, three seconds before the rabbit pushed itself upright. It had one bloodshot eye and one bulging eye. The hole through the animal's skull was higher than where Sergei had aimed, but very close. That shot should've killed the thing.

The left side of the rabbit's face drooped, and bloody saliva spilled from its mouth as it wiggled its nose and jaw. It turned and took a wildly veering step to its left. For its next step, the rabbit attempted to correct the route and meandered to its right before stumbling and falling onto its fluffy furball tail. The motions became more and more jerky by the second as the animal attempted a slow getaway.

Finally, Sergei raised his rifle again. He pulled the bolt and chambered another round. He aimed.

From behind a tipped tree with a large root structure exposed leapt a furry beast. It was brown and lumpy and wrong all over. A bear. One bigger than anything ever seen in Russia. The rabbit was motionless beneath the bear's incredible paws. It sniffed at its quarry and continued sniffing, lifting its snout and turning its face. It looked at the foursome.

Sergei squeezed his trigger.

The bear roared and stiffened. In a blink it was there, only a few feet away. The stench was incredible. It was as if the thing had bathed in fish guts. It opened its mouth to deliver a fresh roar, sending pinked saliva and bits of meat at the men on a backdraft of breath.

Acting on instinct, safeties were released and rounds were chambered. All but Sergei got a shot off as they stumbled in reverse. The bear swung its great, great paw at the man, slicing four matching divots into his abdomen, deep enough to reveal bone and spill guts. He dropped his rifle and tried to hold his body together while greasy, slippery organs oozed out between his fingers.

Buckshot and a .30-06 round drove into the bear's pelt. It flared back in agony before fresh anger had it thrashing at the men with its forepaws. Russell got it the worst, the flesh of his throat torn and flapping as a red, red wash gushed hotly down his front. He was dead within two beats of his heart.

"No, fuck!" Tommy said and pressed his muzzle against the bear's face.

The furry, fleshy cheek blew outward like

Swiss-cheesed rubber. The bear leaned away momentarily before jerking back toward Tommy. Tommy squeezed the trigger again, but he'd emptied the barrels. The bear's great jaws came down over Tommy's head, its snout touching his chest and its chin touching Tommy's shoulder blades. The crunch was fantastic when it bit down. It lifted Tommy and began to shake him, sending out a shower of blood and bone fragments. The grass sparkled with the fresh spillage.

Ilya continued backing up. He was well out of the bear's reach when he re-aimed. Everything below Tommy's upper chest had separated thanks to gravity playing against the tearing bite of the bear. As it chewed through flesh and bone, fluids oozing out from its jaws, Ilya fired.

The shot nailed the target, boring a hole into the bear's face and destroying its left eye. It staggered backward, coughing out great mashed chunks of Tommy. Much of Tommy's face remained together and Ilya made eye contact with his friend.

"Ublyudok!" he shouted.

Ilya pulled the bolt on his rifle. The casing popped and spun on its way to the ground, flickering a golden reflection of the sun. The bear groaned where it lay, and Ilya aimed anew. This round punched up through the beast's chin, changing the shape of its face. It continued to breathe, but those breaths were slow and laboring. Blood bubbled and ran through the hole.

Ilya relaxed some. His body felt emptied, drained. The adrenaline was going as quickly as it had come. He dropped to a knee and closed his eyes. It hit him then. Sergei was gone. They'd grown up in the same town, had been drafted into the WHL as juniors, boarded at the same home, had both tried out for the Abbottsford Heat—back when they were called that—and had both settled for fishing jobs with dreams of owning a gym someday. And then there were Russell and Tommy. He didn't know them as well, but damn, they were good buddies, and—

Ilya screamed, trying to rise. Grey bugs were popping from the dirt and latching onto everything dead, and Ilya's legs. He stumbled, trying to kick away from the scrambling grubs. They weren't overly interested in him and fell away easily, peeling off in glistening swatches. He pushed upright and began running back toward town proper, his eyes glued on the scene. The grey things were dismantling everything and doing so with the celerity of a time-lapse video.

Even while sprinting, he couldn't peel his eyes free…until his right foot slipped into a hole and a bone in his ankle snapped like long-dried kindling.

"Ah! Ublyudok!"

Ilya grimaced, trying to push to his feet. From the ground around him, the grey things began to surface. Broken ankle or not, he couldn't stay there. He scanned for an option. About ten feet away was a mossy boulder with a flat top long enough for him to stretch out upon.

He began to drag himself, never letting go of the rifle. He had one shot left in the magazine and six or seven left in the box in his pocket—at least that many. By the time he reached the rock he was drenched in pain sweat. He pulled himself up. Everywhere he'd been, the grey creatures rose before falling away unfed.

Ilya reached into his pocket for his cellphone, even as he looked at his phone on the ground next to the hole that had tripped him. The grey things were all over it, probably settling for the traces of his being when a full meal wasn't available.

12

Lucy Weight leaned over the counter of the former sewing store, which she'd turned into an entertainment store after receiving the insurance benefits from her husband's life policy. She was watching for the boat. She hadn't had new inventory in almost two weeks and already people were getting a little bored of looking at the scraps left behind when the initial rush filed in during the first few days. She'd been more correct than she could've imagined about Picture Island needing an entertainment store, even with all the people moving away, dying, and being busy with rebuilding what the gator had destroyed. Perhaps it was because of those things that people needed more than a common share of new stuff to look at and play with.

According to the online tracking, she was to receive the massive shipment either two days ago, yesterday, or today. It had new, though remaindered books, comics, stacks of cheap movies, pornography of a few shades, Funko Pops, silk-screened shirts, board games, and numerous used video games for an assortment of systems. She had gotten everything from an American repackaging and print-on-demand company. She had paid almost half as much as the original cost in duty fees and shipping and would still pay less than if she'd bought an identical order from a Canadian company.

Along the sidewalk, Miriam Weever stopped to look at the statue of James and Garth, the heroes of Picture Island—putting the statue up cleared Lucy's conscience concerning the name of her store. Miriam nodded firmly and then stepped inside, a bell jingling above her.

"Hello, a little birdy told me you have *I survived* t-shirts," Miriam said. She was dressed in her typical business finery: pantsuit, smart leather flats, tasteful jewelry.

Lucy cringed. "What size? The tourists snapped most of them up."

"I was thinking of getting one for myself and one for my niece. A medium and a child's small. What exactly do they say?"

"I have the small, but not the medium. I have more coming, should be here any minute, hopefully," Lucy said and then addressed the second part to the question. "They say, *I survived the space gator attack on Picture Island*. I'll show you." Lucy led the real estate agent to the back where she had a single stainless-steel shirt rack—something surprisingly useful left behind amidst all the sewing store junk.

Miriam gave a bemused chuckle. "I think I'd better wait to see if more come in. Everyone at the office will hoot over this."

"You're the real estate lady, yeah?" Lucy said.

Miriam instantly had a business card between two fingers of her left hand—perhaps she'd been a magician in a past life or a gunslinger. “That’s correct. ReMax. There’s a good many listings…I’d actually had the listing for this place a couple years ago, but nobody was biting.”

“Ah.” Lucy looked at the card. “You think all the houses will sell?”

Miriam gave a short, *let me tell you* huff. “I thought it’d all be tourism, a slow trickle in and out. People don’t grasp the remoteness of a place like Picture Island until they’re here a while.”

Lucy gave a nod to this. Every year a handful of new people came and at the same time, last year’s new people packed their stuff.

“So, I figured slowly but surely…well, I got another email today from the secretary of someone famous—first time one came I was like *yeah, right…*I mean so famous I thought it was a hoax. The email looked correct and yada yada yada, but how can you be sure, right?” Miriam took a step to the left to glance through the beaded curtain. “I get a second email from another person, a guy a little higher in the company. He wants to set up a call between me and the famous person.”

“Famous like how?” Lucy said. Miriam looked like she was dying to say it but couldn’t and would dish out a good many clues that would take Lucy to the answer’s doorstep. Hot goss ain’t easy to hold onto.

“It would be too obvious if I said what he does…but he’s not an entertainer. Anyway, finally I get my wits about me and I’m going to put an end to the chicanery. I demand a video call.

Twenty minutes later I get a Zoom link and there he is. In one of his factories, walking and talking. He barely even wanted to know about the properties, he mostly wanted to know about the gator and what happened."

Lucy pieced this together. "Wait, he what, wants to buy the whole town?"

"He has so much money he might buy the whole island. Even with a federal park on it. The uber rich can do anything and he's rich, rich."

"Like top ten in the world?"

Miriam snorted. "I will not confirm or deny that one. I will say this, those guys everyone thought were the military, were only partly right. They're former military turned mercenary, and they work for this guy."

Lucy gazed blankly off to her depleted DVD and Blu-ray section. Now that was some kind of rumor waiting to happen. And if some rich dude tried to buy the whole island, did she move her store? What were mercenaries doing here?

"Let me know if anyone comes in. I'm going to check out *Behind the Green Door;* if you know what I mean. It's bad for business if people see me perusing the adult titles."

"Yeah, no problem," Lucy said and headed for the front and her counter. Behind the counter was a tall stool. She watched out the window. Distantly, making its slow way in, was the ferry from the mainland. "I see the boat. Hopefully my order's on there and we can get you a t-shirt."

13

Once near the island, George sent a text message to Jacy, explaining that he'd been caught by an adult. Jacy didn't respond, which usually meant she was elbow deep in dishwater. George continued with a second message, asking Jacy to have the hideaway location ready for when he finally escaped, and she was off work.

"You hungry?" Lin said.

They were in her Honda HR-V crossover, looking at the back ends of a couple dozen vehicles that had been loaded before her. The radio was set to CBC and a host was talking to two women: one being a woman in Kansas and the other being in Afghanistan. The topic was religious laws imposed to subjugate women's rights by male lawmakers.

"I don't know," George said, and that was true. He didn't know if he was hungry or thirsty or anything else for sure. His mind was cloudy with ideas and half-cooked plans for his immediate future.

"That means you're not too hungry, even if you are hungry. Let's start at the beginning, at Josie Kincaid's home where you'd come to best the gator without quite finishing it off."

George shrugged at this. The longer this

woman spent not calling the hospital, the longer he felt he had to work out a plan of escape. Though she'd already told him she would ship him away first thing tomorrow.

"I don't want to get the days mixed up in my head. You went back to the cottage, right? The cottage is kind of the home base for where people fully started to understand?"

The boat hit its rubber bumpers against the dock's rubber bumpers with a hollow *bong*. Men and women in safety vests moved around busily, retrieving chock blocks, tossing ropes, and standing near control panels. An engine rumbled to life and steel wench cables screeched as the nose of the ferry was lifted from the hull to allow a passable plane for drivers.

"No. Only for me. The first night everybody already knew and chased it up to Josie's. We were in bed, inside," George said, watching the slow activity around them.

"Right. And the second night you went up to get comic books, correct?"

George nodded.

Directly ahead of them, vehicles began to start engines. The rumble of it within the steel hull overpowered the women on the radio. The sky far above was overcast and threatening rain. Weather on Picture Island was unpredictable and often violent, though good or bad, the extremes never stuck around long.

"About a million years ago I covered a comic book convention. I met a guy trying to sell a set of the first twenty issues of Action Comics for three million bucks. All the really key Superman issues. Superman couldn't fly or see through walls until issue ten or eleven—I don't recall exactly. The twentieth issue was where they introduced Lex Luther, which I guess is the final key of the earliest ones. He didn't get it, and if he held onto them these last fifteen years, he'd probably get triple what he'd originally wanted." Lin let out an amused huff. "He couldn't even show inside because they were graded. Imagine buying a comic you couldn't even look at."

George knew she was trying to warm to him. He was quiet and thoughtful enough to know some of the games adults played. Kids played them, too. Especially girls when they wanted to get a boy in trouble with a teacher.

"I like horror comics," he said.

Lin started her engine and put it into gear as soon as the vehicle in front of them began to move. They rolled slowly, crossing the steel drawbridge. Raindrops had begun pattering the windows. Despite the impending weather, Picture Island was busy with tourist activity.

"Ah, I know little about horror. Not quite as important to my editors I suppose, since I've never been assigned anything horror entertainment," Lin said.

They continued following traffic until reaching a stop sign.

"Left," George said. "I only knew to get the gator under the scale because of a horror comic."

Lin turned and followed a three-vehicle parade through a loosely residential area and to another stop sign. Both vehicles ahead took right turns. Lin looked at George, eyebrows raised.

"Follow this all the way to the end. It goes to the hot springs."

"You don't remember the name and issue number of the comic, do you?"

"*Unexpected*, but I don't know which one."

"*Unexpected?* Is that the name?" Lin said.

George nodded.

"I bet we can find the covers on Google and can play police lineup."

George shrugged.

The rain remained a steady, slow patter, even beneath the canopy of branches twining fingers high above the road. The asphalt ended suddenly, and they bumped down. The world started to close in around the vehicle.

Lin reached back between the seats to a canvas bag and unzipped a pocket. She withdrew a digital voice recorder. She tapped the power button on the radio before holding the recorder up to her mouth.

"Beyond town it's quick to find wilderness. It's a quiet, lonely place that is surely crawling with life just below the surface. Though the tracks are gone, my mind's eye can see the deep grooves left by the creature's sharp claws. I can see the deep, deep divot that dragging its immensity down to town dug into the dirty gravel road." Lin paused, a thinking expression upon her face. "The road is forever thinning, as if down a throat. The forest is a mouth. At the end of this path, I'll see where nature devoured so many before taking the show…before taking the feast to the town Ghost Clearing."

Lin lowered the recorder. Nodding, eyes hazy and thoughtful as she stared through the windshield. George understood how she could be a podcast personality. He wished when he talked it came out smart like that.

They wound the final turn preceding Josie's short laneway. George pointed out the window. "That's Josie's," he said.

The rain was coming a bit faster now as Lin pulled into the lane and beneath a less obscured sky. Locals had scavenged the wreckage for materials, and tourists scavenged for mementos. Lin put down her window and they listened to the thrum of the forest.

"The tour group stops here. The people in charge told me the guests don't touch anything, but that's a lot of footprints leading to the door."

George nodded. The proofs of human contact were varied and abundant.

Lin lifted the recorder to begin a fresh bout of atmospheric description. Distantly, the ferry's airhorn sounded its departure. George listened as he looked out the window to the mess. At least he'd made it and Lin hadn't sent him back on the first ship away.

14

Denver went to his room after receiving the map from Mandy. He changed into gear better suited for a nature hike. He was almost out the door when he thought better of hitting the wilderness without at least making an attempt on the can. Eating restaurant food for every meal had made his functions erratic.

While seated with his pants and underwear around his calves, he got to imagining fantastical possibilities beyond that the gator had brought along a stowaway slug—he didn't really buy the deer thing and guessed that Mandy would be permanently seeing overlarge animals as a side-effect of surviving the giant gator-like creature's attacks.

He then began to look to outlandish ideas. What if the creature changed the island's genetic path by simple proximity? As if to survive a giant, all the island's other animals also had to become giants: evolve in a flash or risk being wiped out. It sounded impossible, but nature often found a way. Not long ago he'd read an article about elephants being born without tusks, evolving to be less attractive to poachers. Brains were incredible machines, and he didn't dare try to assume to know what was truly possible or not…though he'd always play it cautiously when speaking aloud.

"One slug…but also some large larva," he said,

musing.

Given that evolutionary changes didn't happen overnight, or in a matter of weeks, what *really* might've caused this? It looked like a black slug, just huge and deformed. That alone would feel more like a singular event. But the feasting larva, how had they gotten so large? He closed his eyes, *seeing* mutating agents travel the bloodstream of the island's fauna. What was the step earlier? Had the creature secreted something into the soil? When they blew it up, did it vaporize and become an aerosol that lingered in the forest like a growth fog?

"You're being ridiculous," he said.

Outside, he stretched his back. Spittle freckled his forehead. He turned back and retreated to his room for his windbreaker jacket. He was unrushed. This situation was far from an emergency.

He put up his hood before exiting the front doors of the Picture House Lodge and headed in the direction of the map. There were about ten minutes of town walking to do before reaching the trail Mandy had followed into the forest. Though unmarked by a sign, footfalls clearly labeled the path into the woods. For the first chunk, the trees were close and tight, but beyond, things thinned. Great empty knolls with soggy, mossy floors filled in the gaps between patches of forest. The skies opened up a little more and the raindrops thickened. If he'd had anything else to do, he might've turned around. As it was, he was now only killing time, looking for a final fantastic *something* to happen.

"Help."

Denver paused, listening. The rain hitting his hood was loud enough that he had to question if he'd heard anything at all. He put down his hood and rain began to work at flattening his hair.

"Help."

Directly ahead of Denver was a small patch of trees. He began following the trail around them and toward one of many clearings in this patch of woods.

"Help."

There was no question he was hearing something. He rounded the trees and scanned the semi-vacancy of the space.

"Help."

There, maybe twenty feet from where he stood, was a man on a rock. He lay as if marooned there. He was waving his left arm in lazy strokes, as if worn out.

"Hey!" Denver said and began jogging.

The man sat up straighter and craned around to scan the clearing before turning to again look at Denver. "You have a cellphone? Call for help, now!"

Denver automatically reached into his pocket. "What happened?" he said. He was now spitting distance from the man, and he'd quite obviously broken his leg or possibly only his ankle. The ugliness of the angle wasn't severe but there was no way it could carry weight.

"There was big, big bear and then huge maggot things came out of the ground. They taste blood and want more!"

The man was pale and visibly shaken, while visibly shaking. All over he moved, as if on the natural vibration of distress.

Knowing what he knew about Ghost Clearing and the rest of Picture Island, rather than dialling 911, he called the hotel. Most of the emergency service crew of volunteers was dead, but Mandy would know who else to call. Denver turned to look at the man while the line rang in his ear.

"Where's the bear?" he said.

"They ate it. It was biggest bear I see and they ate it like nothing! The maggots! They ate all the corpses! The bear ate Sergei!"

"Calm down, I'm—hey, Mandy. Denver here. I found an injured man out near where you sent me. Can you get someone to come out with an ATV and a wagon, or one of those six-wheelers?"

Denver stepped a dozen or so feet over to strange white growths, assuming they were mushrooms while Mandy spoke in his ear. He knelt.

"Yeah, he's got a Russian accent." Denver lowered his voice. "Says a bear got…" he trailed as he nudged the not-mushroom with a knuckle. It was a claw. He shoved it harder. "Holy cow."

"The maggots, they drag bones under that moss."

Denver looked at the man as he answered a question Mandy had asked. "No, he says Sergei is dead." Two seconds later, he said, "You're Ilya?"

The man nodded as Denver straightened up. He began kicking at the loose, mossy carpet, revealing terrifyingly large bones, including a skull that was as big as a beach ball and then some.

A giddy trill played up from his stomach as he said, “I think something is happening out here. Something incredible, even by Picture Island standards.”

15

Jacy sat on the clean, stainless-steel counter in her kitchen whites, munching on a plate of fries with ketchup. She'd finished all the dishes from the lunch rush and had about an hour until the first supper dishes would come in. The special was a soup and Jacy eyed the scum line in the huge pot from a distance. That wouldn't be the worst of it, tomorrow morning there'd be a dozen or more little bowls specifically made for the soup; melted and dried cheese would be rimming these bowls. The cheese would come off easily enough, but it would linger in the water in great, rubbery chunks that caught up between her fingers and made her shiver all over at the grossness.

Dishes at a restaurant was a lot harder than dishes at home.

Settled, she turned on her phone. She'd discovered on her first day that she couldn't get anything done if it was on all the time, it was simply too tempting. She only turned it on during breaks, and even then, tried not to use it the whole time on account of how quickly the breaks seemed to slip away.

Today had been tough to stick to the rule. With George coming, the world seemed to slow down, and she found herself eyeing the clock on the wall to the left of the sink every seven or eight minutes. One time she made it twelve minutes; certain it had been at least half an hour.

"Uh oh," she said upon reading George's three long text messages.

Before coming to the hotel, she'd scoped out a few of the places with for sale signs and picked the one that looked easiest to break into. The gator must've gone by it because the back porch was smashed in, and the door had only plastic covering it. Inside was all the furniture George would need, for however long he was staying. She figured once her parents were let off the cruise, they'd come get her and she'd convince them that George was an orphan and had saved her life, then they'd have to adopt him—not legally, of course. She thought she'd make George pretend to be gay so they weren't funny about him moving in. And then once she was old enough, they'd reveal the truth and announce the impending wedding. Simple.

She like, liked George a lot and figured she'd love him, by and by. He was a hero after all, and he didn't mind that she talked all the time. Most people got mad at her for talking.

She typed a reply to George:

Don't worry. I know where you can stay and nobody will find you.

She hadn't told George of the long-term plan, but knew he'd go along with it because that was his nature. She would lead him, and he would follow happily behind her.

16

George finally got a text message back from Jacy and it instantly buoyed his mental state. He'd worried greatly about Carole's friend, though more so, he wanted to be with Jacy. Spending time face to face was infinitely better than chatting on Zoom.

Lin was walking over the rubble of Josie's home, talking into her voice recorder. George waited, wondering if they were going to drive to the hot springs or walk the path of destruction that connected to two points. He guessed walk, but she'd left the hatch of the Honda open, so he couldn't be certain.

George watched and Lin finally seemed to recall his presence. She came back over to him, nodding as she walked.

"Some situation. Will you talk me through what happened, maybe where the gator had been and how it came onto the property?"

George gave a curt nod and started across the yard to the destroyed trees. The pale, yellowy innards beneath the bark looked fresh, as if they might've been revealed that morning and not two weeks ago. Lin followed, holding her recorder a foot from his face.

"It chased after people. They were coming to Josie's door, trying to get away. The trees crashed and people were going crazy..." George went as in-depth as his memory served before getting to how he came to shoot the gator in just the right spot. He'd told this to Lin already, over Zoom, but he liked telling it. It was exciting and proved the undeniable value of horror comics.

Lin pointed the recorder back to her face. "The destruction is incredible. In breadth, one might imagine a tank rumbling through the woods rather than an animal. The disregard for full-sized trees is mystifying. The immense power revealed in the creature's aftermath is enough to give goosebumps."

She lowered the recorder and scanned the trees a moment longer. Not far from where they stood, amid the thick foliage, something began moving. It was a forest, and though both looked, they lost interest whenever whatever was in there didn't present itself.

"The hot springs are close by foot? I think I can hear them," Lin said.

George nodded again and started off. The path was ten times wider than the first time he'd been on it.

"The clearness of the creature's movements is astounding, even these weeks later. I can imagine the incredible cacophony of sound, the scattering of debris, the general chaos of its hunger. It's truly astounding," Lin said into the recorder.

The dirt became the clay-mud that mixed with gravel beneath the mossy floor surrounding the pools of steamy water. George stopped walking before crossing the invisible line that marked where the forest stopped and the springs began.

There was a thick, silver web, only visible thanks to the rain that had collected. It was impossibly thick and yet melded in with the scenery: a perfect trap.

George put his hand out a second too late to stop Lin's forward motion. She came into contact, as the hand with the voice recorder touched the web, sending out a shimmering spray of rainwater. She pulled back and found her arm stuck.

"What's this?" Lin said. She looked up and down, and then began yanking with renewed vigor. "I'm stuck."

George was way ahead of her, imagining the size of the spider that had produced such a web. His mind immediately bounced to a story he'd read in a comic called *Creepy Things* about a swamp and…gators were from swamps; did it somehow bring along a swamp spider?

He swallowed an invisible ball as he scanned the world. He took a step to his right, seeing then the nose of the Audi. The cellphone on the ground. The beer bottles next to the first pool. Then he looked up.

"Oh no," he whispered.

Hanging upside down were at least six human-sized forms and three that were obviously massive deer. Each was encapsulated by white spiderweb. The human faces were visible and one of them was deeply red, almost purple, while the others had gone ghostly pale, as if exsanguinated.

"Look," he whispered, mouth close to Lin's shoulder.

She quit struggling and looked. And saw. She

began struggling harder. From way, way up a tree, a spider rocketed down on a strand of webbing.

"Help me!"

George began pulling at her hips as she peeled off her sweater. Her hand remained stuck, no matter how hard they jerked and yanked and grunted. He tried to think of other spider scenarios and the only weapon that ever seemed to work was a torch.

"Fire?" he said.

Lin blinked at him, one eye still on the spider now barreling toward them. "Two road flares. In the trunk. In the safety kit."

George broke off into a sprint, back to the Honda. Lin wailed in terror behind him. He passed the rubble of Josie's home and the bush that had shaken when they'd walked by just a minute earlier, not daring to look for fear of what might emerge. He heard rustling but was already running as fast as he could go.

The Honda came into view, as did a frog the size of a big dog. It was in the shotgun seat. George slowed. Lin's wailing had stopped, which had to be a bad sign. Once to the bumper, the frog lashed out its tongue. The windshield became a white fog of shattered but still whole, safety glass. George let out a squeak and continued toward the yawning hatch. Just inside the open door, within a stretchy net compartment was an orange tackle box with the word EMERGENCY written in a bulky, army stencil font.

Up front, the frog shattered the glass. It became aware of George's new position after thumping onto the hood. The slick pink tongue fired out between the seats. Saliva sprayed from its tip onto George's nose, but nothing more—he was less than an inch out of reach. He yanked the kit out of the Honda and started to run again.

He heard the monstrous frog chasing behind him, but a new worry entered the picture. A garter snake as big as a horror flick anaconda slithered out from the shrub they'd seen moving earlier. George barked out a fresh gasp, skirting far to his left across Josie's yard. The snake didn't seem interested in him, however, and when he glanced back, he saw why. The frog tried to stop in the rain-slick grass and slipped as it attempted a 180° turn. The snake was lightning quick and grabbed the frog between its fantastic jaws.

George stumbled onward. He'd quit running to open the tackle box without dropping it. He made it a handful of steps, juggling the contents of the box, before spilling everything. He dropped to his knees. Amid the non-perishable crackers and the packets of peanut butter and the first-aid bag and the mini traffic pylons and the little heat pads were two orange road flares. He grabbed them and then looked at Lin, or rather, where Lin had been. She was gone, so was that piece of spiderweb. He craned his head and there she was, looking dopey in expression, as if drugged, and hanging upside down. She'd been wrapped, a snack for later. The spider was a few feet from her and coming for George.

He dropped the flares and pulled out his cellphone. He had to call someone, or at least text

Jacy. No service. He looked above the screen and the spider was right there. From its mandibles, two fine pricks jutted out and George instinctively tossed his cellphone at the spider. The needle tips punctured the phone, and a burst of battery acid splashed the spider's mouth. It keened a high wail before retreating in pain. Over and over, George's only real advantage against giant beasts was that they always underestimated him and his luck.

The snake was in Josie's driveway, the frog a lump in its throat. Beyond it on the roof of the Honda, as if gauging their chances, were two more enormous frogs.

George couldn't go that way. He also couldn't stay put. He looked to the shrub where the snake had been. At least the snake wasn't interested in him, meaning it was unlikely that more frogs hung out down there. The only problem was where to go after that.

A frog cried out.

George knelt and snatched at the orange cylinders before he jumped to his feet, a road flare in each hand. He ran to the edge of the overgrown lawn and looked down over the shrubbery. The hill was fairly steep, but manageable. At the bottom was a creek. The road wound over a handful of creeks along the way, he had to hope he'd be lucky enough that this was one of those creeks.

He reached the edge and stuffed the flares into his pockets. He turned, hoping to go down nice and easy on his fours. His right foot slipped, and then his left. His palms dragged along the sharp grass as he slid. He tried to hug himself to the hillside but failed and began rolling. *Thump! Thump!* He continued barreling to the edge of the creek and came to a stop against a boulder with another heavy *thump!* that knocked the wind from his lungs and left him gasping for breath.

After thirty seconds of helplessness, he felt his pockets. He had the flares and despite some forthcoming bruises, the resiliency of youth left his body unharmed. Up to his feet, he got to walking.

17

As Mandy stood by the front desk, wondering who in the hell she'd call for help, a foursome of fishermen stepped in the lobby doors of the hotel. They'd obviously already had a long day. They looked exhausted. Gear wet and dirty, cheeks rosy, eyes puffy. They were newish to the island, having only been there about ten months. They'd been out to sea during the gator attacks.

"You. There's been an accident. A man has a broken leg. A bear attack," Mandy said.

The man in the lead sighed with his entire body.

"Free pound of wings each and two pitchers of beer. This is serious."

Mandy understood the reluctance. These weren't people who'd grown up here. These weren't even people who did all that much shopping or eating in Ghost Clearing. They just happened to work off the private docks.

"Yeah, all right," another of the men said. He was big everywhere but above the shoulders. His head was totally unbefitting of his body.

Mandy had the manpower, all she needed now was to think of somewhere to borrow horsepower. It hit her then. The late Henry Weight had had an ATV and trailer, and unless Lucy sold it... She scooped up the phone and dialed Lucy's cell from memory.

Lucy answered on the second ring and Mandy said, "You still have Henry's ATV? We've got an emergency out in the woods."

Lucy said she did, and that Mandy could borrow anything she liked from the garage. Mandy ordered the fishermen to follow her after she grabbed up her long rifle. As she walked, rifle in her armpit, she sent a text message to Denver Jones, suddenly feeling guilty about sharing her discovery with him.

18

At Ilya's insistence, Denver went searching for one of the other weapons that had to be around there somewhere. He found Sergei's rifle after some gentle digging with the toes of his boots and attempted to hand it over to Ilya where he remained stranded on the rock.

"No, you," Ilya said. "I have mine. Fire it to see if it works."

Denver pointed it at the ground a yard from where they were and squeezed the trigger. Nothing happened.

"You must pull lever for the bolt to expel spent casing. You never shoot rifle before?" Ilya said. Despite being terribly overwrought, the condescension and disbelief were thick on his words.

"Yes, I have, as a matter of fact," Denver said.

He did as told. He closed the chamber and fired into the ground. The shot echoed in every direction.

"How many cartridge?"

"How do I check?" Denver said, looking at the rifle from a side angle, as if there might be a display window somewhere.

"In bottom, in front of trigger guard."

Denver saw it and popped the stubby magazine

free. "One, looks like."

"Here," Ilya said after reaching into his pocket for the crumbled ammo box he'd brought along. "Fill magazine and put one in chamber."

It took a few seconds for Denver to understand what Ilya meant by putting one in the chamber after filling the magazine. He popped the spent round and inserted a fresh one rather than forcing the bolt to lever one in place. He straightened and stood with the rifle. It was almost like an out of body experience, being there with this strange Russian and the bones of a massive bear. It was all so insane, part of his logical mind had checked out and in its place was a gulley awaiting an adrenaline rush, another new discovery.

To kill the silence and break up the monotony of waiting, Denver said, "So, what brought you to Canada?"

"Hockey," Ilya said. "I should have stayed in Russia maybe, but KGB disappeared my father and brother and Sergei and me had opportunity in junior to get away."

"Geez, that's awful."

Ilya shrugged. "They were campaigning for Gennady Zyuganov. My mother say they should have known better. Yeltsin was same as Putin is now. He gets all the vote he want and make sure nobody else get vote enough to oppose."

"That's hard to believe, in this day and age," Denver said, though it was much easier to believe than everything that had happened on Picture Island.

Ilya snorted. "Is the way most places. I like

Canada. Good elections. I almost went to play in Switzerland, hockey team asked me and Sergei after first season in AHL. But Europe is very close to Russia. I'd rather be fisherman than disappeared hockey player."

Denver knew nothing about hockey, or Canadian elections, or how far a Russian dictator might reach to snuff out a loose end despite it not being *his* loose end. Likely it was excessive precaution, but who knew, even dictators could be petty.

"You are scientist, yes?"

Denver nodded. "I'm an astronomer. I chased down the meteorite that appears to have been a frozen egg, which may or may not have housed the gator-like creature that ravished the island."

Ilya snorted. "If not from space, where the hell did it come from?"

Denver didn't want to argue that not being indigenous to an area did not automatically mean it was from a specific elsewhere, no matter the circumstantial evidence, no matter the likelihoods, no matter the suggestive, inconclusive DNA evidence. He didn't want to argue at all. He wanted it to be from space and for there to be more where it came from. The secrets a living specimen would tell…

"The real question is how one giant creature has become multiple giant creatures," Denver said.

"No. Question is, how much will it hurt on bumpy ATV with broken ankle?" Ilya said.

Denver opened his mouth to reply but snapped

it closed. Distantly, an ATV engine buzzed, coming nearer, suggesting this little interlude was going to be rather eventless for Denver.

"Dorogoy bog na nebesakh," Ilya said and lifted his rifle, aiming behind Denver as he placidly watched for the oncoming ATV in another direction.

19

George was now steady on his feet—he'd had to pause when he'd first climbed upright as dizziness hit him. He gave his body a quick feel as if he might find something broken that had gone unfelt, and then continued off in the general direction the road would've followed far above. The creek was loud enough that it presented a false sense of safety. That water seemed normal, so George watched it more than he watched his feet…until he stepped on a slug the size of a football and nearly slipped into the creek as the innards gushed out of the smooshed bug like gear grease.

"Ugh!" he said.

He tried to kick away the gunk, tried to rub it free against the grass. It was almost as if the dead slug had adhered to his sneaker. Almost as if it were still alive and clinging for survival. The creek was fast, and it wasn't cool enough that a soaker would bother his already wet foot, so he dunked the dirty shoe in and shook the slug around. Bits of the slug began to break away.

George gasped.

He'd had no time to act. A four-foot yelloweye fish with a mouth big enough to engulf his shoe sideways had latched onto his foot. He fell back into the grassy edge and tried to kick, but the fish was too, too heavy.

"Let go!"

Its great back fin stretched high out of the water like something prehistoric. George jerked and spun, trying to shake the thing before it took his foot. It suddenly left off and his shoe was clean. He brought both sopping feet to the grass and lay back a moment, catching his breath.

George had gone fishing twice with his father, before he'd died in a car accident and George had been shipped off to live with Carole and Shane—long before Shane hung himself in the garage. His father had caught two trout the first time and three useless sunfish the second time. That massive yelloweye that had sucked the slug from his boot was the first fish George had ever caught. And really, it had caught him.

He mused over this only a minute or so, until his breathing was back to neutral. He rolled to his knees and looked into the long, windblown grass a few feet from the muddy creekbank. Eyes peered back at him. Almost as slimy in appearance as the black slug, a salamander as big as a pug dog stood dead still. Slowly, cautiously, George pushed to his feet and began stepping backward. The salamander crept from the grass and followed him, matching his pace.

"No, you stay. Stay."

The salamander wasn't listening, didn't understand, didn't care most likely.

"Git!"

George looked around for something to throw and considered lighting a flare. He decided against it. Something told him this creature was only curious and that more trouble, bigger trouble, would lie in wait for him further along the path—like one of those damned spiders.

From the far side of the creek came a rustling. The salamander immediately forgot about George and bolted back into the tall grass. Clumsy though speedy, a duck the size of a big, big swan trudged through the mud and shrubs on the far side and plopped down into the creek, sending out a splash like a warning shot across the bow. George and the bird shared eye-contact until the duck honked a tremendous squawk and George bolted.

20

Ilya fired the shot and Denver turned. For a heartbeat, he was certain the injured Russian had lost his mind and was firing on him. His life did not flash before his eyes. Instead, he saw himself at the beach arcade with his cousin Rita. They played *Area 51* almost religiously all summer. She was fourteen and he was fifteen. On the morning he was to leave, they headed down to the arcade only to discover the *Area 51* machine was occupied by two grown men. Rather than play something else, they walked under the pier, wordlessly, as if there had only ever been two options, and fooled around. He had to jump into the ocean to hide the wet spots in his shorts and on his shirt. She jumped in to make it look normal that he was soaked when they went back to her house.

Denver had erased the embarrassing incident from his mind, but here it was, dug fresh like a grave near a nineteenth century medical school. Of course, the shot didn't kill him because Ilya was shooting beyond at impossible beasts.

Four coyotes the size of Fiats had crawled from shallow burrows and were charging toward them. Ilya's shot missed its target. He fired again. The poor angle of his body had his sights all crooked.

"Shoot!" Ilya shouted.

Denver brought his rifle up to just beneath his

chin and squeezed the trigger. The coyotes were now close enough that they were virtually impossible to miss. Denver's shot sent one of the coyotes spinning and yipping. The rifle's recoil hammered into his chin, instantly blacking his vision like a perfect punch.

Ilya kept firing until he was squeezing at nothing. Denver heard the shots and then swearing, but also heard the oncoming ATV. A coyote latched onto Denver's knee and he jerked upright at the waist. He punched and tried to kick, but the coyote was too big and willful, dragging him over the soft mossy floor of the forest. It was nearly too late when he thought of the rifle. He spun at the hips and reached back, grabbed the hot barrel and pulled the weapon to his chest as the beast continued dragging him.

On the rock, Ilya was being mauled and shaken. He was shouting in Russian and screaming in the universal language of terrorized pain. Denver couldn't worry about that and chambered a round. He fired into the neck of the coyote chewing on him. It let up and skittered in reverse. The first coyote he'd shot was back and Denver began to panic. He jerked at the bolt and rammed it back in place so hard that he fired the round.

Into his foot.

The bottom half of his boot was gone and what remained was a stringy mess of roasted flesh and white, white bone. He fainted dead away. Dual coyote bites brought him back and he wailed as they feasted on the mangled meat and boot leather.

“Holy shit!” Mandy shouted over the gentle rumble of the ATV.

Her huge rifle began to buck off shots that echoed in a way that seemed to shake the forest at its core. The biting ceased and a hot, hot spill of coyote blood poured onto Denver. He looked down, making eye-contact with a dead beast. Its tongue drooped grotesquely. One of its ears had been blown clean away. There was no rise or fall of its great breast.

“Ilya! Ilya!” Mandy screamed.

Denver lay back, thinking of his cousin. He’d seen her once since, at a wedding. Even more than a decade after the fact, it had been awkward as hell.

“Denver, you alive?” Mandy said.

The grey sky above opened a little further and the rain fell harder. He stuck out his tongue. He was parched from screaming and terribly thirsty in general.

“Yes,” he said, or thought he said.

Denver blinked in and out of consciousness for the entire bumpy trip back to the hotel.

21

Lin came to with an immense pressure in her sinus. She was hanging way above the hot springs pools, wrapped tightly in webbing. She was still dopey on the spider's poison, but she had enough of her wits to deny the urge to close her eyes again. She looked around. The woman to her right was grey, her lips blue, and quite obviously dead. She looked left and the spider was there, its face buried in the silk of the feeding cocoon. The man next to the woman was still alive, though his formerly purple face was now pale and paling further by the second as the huge insect had its fill.

Lin forced herself to play it cool. It wasn't easy. Seeing this horrible act up close and personal like this made her want to smoke. She could smoke, if she could get to her pocket and then from the pack to her mouth with a cigarette. After that all she'd have to do was touch the tip of the torch lighter she'd…the thought trailed, forming into a plan of sorts.

The man next to her began gagging. Saliva was sticky around his lips and much of his face was starting to cave in on itself. It seemed the spider was taking more than blood. And she was almost certainly next.

And she'd never see June again.

Or Trina, or Conrad, or Devon.

And her sweet, sweet baby June would grow up without ever really knowing her mother.

Fuck that.

Lin inched her hand to her pocket. The lump was there within the material of her pants, and her being turned upside down had the cigarettes and lighter slipping free. She ran her index finger against the smooth steel paddle. All she had to do was get the lighter turned around and begin to burn. She couldn't place where she'd picked up the factoid, but regular spiderwebs began to burn at only 50-60°C—much, much cooler than the flame of a torch lighter. Even these webs, as thick and sticky as they were, couldn't withstand a torch flame, surely.

The spider continued feeding well after the man's body ceased any movement and had run out of color. A raindrop played down over Lin's chin as she watched. She hadn't noticed the weather and right then decided the rain had damned well better stay out of her way, or else.

Ginger and patient, she turned the lighter until it faced out. Now, she only had to wait for a little space between herself and the giant spider feeding on the man. She refused to acknowledge the thought that the spider might not be alone, that it might be part of some spider gang. The Sharks and the Jets and the Spiders; she was becoming undone.

She closed her eyes and June's chubby little face rose like a full moon in a werewolf flick. A funny thought, mixing her sweet baby with a monster. Any urge to laugh departed as all the humor in the world had dried up. The spider seemed to be looking at her, though without mammalian pupils, she really couldn't tell for certain. From somewhere below, though beyond her vantage, branches snapped. The spider turned its attention, retracting its face from the dregs of its meal. More snapping cracked a soundtrack over the bubbling of the hot springs and the gentle patter of rain. The spider was sluggish as it attempted to scurry away.

Lin could not afford to care what was down there. She pressed the paddle that put the lighter's mechanisms into play. She smelled it before she had visual confirmation that it was working. That scent: fine cotton left beneath an iron too long.

Her hand was suddenly free. The cigarettes dropped and the lighter nearly did as well. She barely caught it, the tip hot in her palm. She winced. She repositioned the lighter in her damp grip and blindly tried to keep the burn flowing. Her arm below the elbow was free and she pointed the flame directly at her middle. Within seconds she felt the warmth accompanied by the releasing pressure that held her tight.

Her arm came high and now she saw the webbing burn. Like woven strands of tissue paper, but crackly with moisture and layered several dozen times.

Below, something splashed into one of the hot springs. No matter what, she couldn't worry about this, despite that something large had gone into the pool where she'd land. Whatever it was, it couldn't matter; to stay in the tree was to be sucked dry as a November leaf. She kept burning.

The webbing remained like a weighted backpack where she couldn't reach, but otherwise, her upper half was free. She forced a sit-up—thankful for the cardio and core classes she took three nights a week at Curves. A groan escaped her mouth as she held the pose, trying for her feet and beyond.

The spider caught her movement and despite whatever was below, decided the risk was worthy. It charged at her, rocking the now loose hold of her body. She straightened, took a breath, and bent back to her legs, making a tight U of her body. They were free to her ankles at the front. A sticky swatch covered most of her backside, top to bottom.

"Come on!" she grunted, bending her knees as she reached, reached, reached.

The spider was a foot away and fired a fresh web. The web holding Lin was much, much thicker than the rest, but that only delayed the burn by a couple seconds. It snapped and Lin began to crash. The fresh web attached to her chest momentarily stopped her motion before whiplashing the spider down with her. She landed in the first pool and the spider landed next to the second. She fell to a depth much deeper than expected and screamed into the pool when she saw the incredible snake coiled down there.

She jerked herself upright. The spider chased her motion. She gasped a great breath once possible. The spider was at the lip of the pool, its weepy fangs itching to tear into her. The two needles within its mandible flared outward, secreting droplets of clear fluid. Lin was in the process of jerking away when the snake launched itself, jaws gaping, onto the spider.

The spider's furry legs wriggled, kicking up mud and dirt, while the snake attempted to swallow. It was the most incredible wildlife moment she'd ever seen but she wasn't sticking around to see how it played out.

Her feet found a shallow platform within the pool as she pushed up to the ledge. She rolled onto solid ground, sopping and exhausted. The spiderweb remained on her back and the backs of her legs. She shuffled and kicked. The stuff refused to tear.

There, in the hoofprint of something so big she didn't want to imagine what it might be, was the lighter. It was wet. She pressed the paddle three times before the blue flame leapt from the tip. She carved the webbing until she had two legs and was about to pocket the lighter when she saw her cigarette pack. It was soaked and yawning open, but maybe, just maybe she'd get lucky.

All the paper had gone mostly translucent, but for two of the cigarettes—they were the final two from the smaller of the decks. She slipped both free, one went between her lips while the other went over her right ear. She lit and inhaled.

As she sat there, regaining her mental equilibrium, she shot a single glance back to the snake. All but the butt of the spider had been engulfed. She ran to the road and kept going, seeing her Honda like a lighthouse through a fog bank.

22

The scary stuff seemed behind him. He'd gotten used to seeing and stepping over the slugs. The ducks ignored him. That salamander had followed him a while, but it appeared he was a curiosity to the lizard and nothing more. The fish were a non-concern as he stayed on land. He'd gone close to half an hour and was now certain that any minute he'd reach the road and be able to run back to town with a fresh story to tell—he might even get there in time to save the reporter woman, though he doubted it.

After another three minutes of winding along with the creek, an incline presented itself. The creek veered away hard and then through a steel culvert. George was positive the road lay atop the incline.

He charged, ready to lean on hands and knees for balance. He got one, two, three crawling steps before the ground disappeared beneath him. Sand and stone dropped as George did. His hands grasped and his arms swung, pinwheeling in the air. His legs kicked at nothing. He landed hard, again.

This time, his ankles and tailbone took the brunt and his breathing, though rushed, moved from his chest with ease. From the bottom, as he rubbed his stinging feet, George looked to a sky that seemed miles upon miles away. All around him, beyond where the light reached, was a mystery shrouded by darkness.

He heard things. Chittering noises.

He patted around the floor of the hole after touching his empty pockets. He'd dropped the flares. The chittering sounds drew closer. Panic began to set in. George crawled, blindly tapping for his lost lights. The floor was pebbly dirt. Some areas were smoothed over, as if polished.

He felt the cool, hard cylinder and pawed for the top as he shuffled sideways, back into the light. He got the end off with a grunt and the flare lit instantly. He hadn't expected it to be so simple and it jumped from his grip. It rolled across the floor, and he chased after it. It came to rest against a wall that appeared to have been carved by rudimentary tools of some fashion. He picked up the flare and went in search of the second flare. The chamber wasn't all that big. He'd passed right over the other flare at some point in his blind search, certainly.

The chittering couldn't be more than ten feet from where he stood, but the source remained hidden in the shadows. George plucked the second flare and put it into his back pocket. There was no way up, he had to look for a way out. For the obvious reason, he moved away from the chittering and discovered a tunnel, one that he could crouch-walk through. He gave a single look back, huffed, and then carried forward.

He shuffled through the tunnel for less than a

minute before another carved chamber opened and he discovered a wall with three more tunnels. Everything appeared to move downward, which was the ultimate goal, he supposed—getting down the hill was getting down the hill, aboveground or below. Perhaps these tunnels connected with whatever kind of sewer system they had on Picture Island.

Then again, the tunnels weren't manmade.

His mind wandered as he decided the methodical choice was best. He'd stick to the right, and if that didn't work, he'd retreat and choose another path; so long as that chittering behind him didn't get any closer. There'd be no backtracking if whatever made that noise cut him off.

The righthand tunnel was tighter than the tunnel he'd come through, but there was still plenty of room for his 4'7" and 75 pounds. Also, plenty of room for the slugs he'd seen…but they weren't big enough and they didn't make the kind of noises that were now coming up from behind him. So, what had made the tunnels? He imagined the kinds of worms that littered horror comics. They usually had strangely humanoid faces with drooly mouths and teeth like a piranha. Did worms chitter? He didn't think so.

He shook his head to rid the images and tried to keep up his speed. It would do him absolutely zero good to imagine that all the creatures that lived underground had somehow been giganticized. No doubt it all had to do with the space gator, but how? In those old comics the typical conclusion would've been a mad scientist or a nuclear explosion. Neither fit this situation.

"Doesn't matter," he whispered, reaffirming his need to focus while distracting himself from just how big that chittering was getting.

He cleared the tunnel and spilled into the next chamber, falling three feet to the ground. The flare stabbed into the dirt floor and went out. He sat there a moment in the complete dark. His hearing seemed to heighten, and his nose started picking up the scent of raw meat. He said a silent prayer that the meat scent was a simple case of extreme paranoia.

He felt into his pocket for the second flare. It lit and his head leveled out. He'd been exaggerating, almost hallucinating, surely. There were five options for progression. This time he went to the far left tunnel. He took a deep inhalation through his nose. Everything smelled like dirt now. He turned his left ear and plugged his right. This tunnel sounded empty.

As good as any other option, this was to be his direction.

After forty or so steps, the tunnel began to close in, and a wall appeared before him. No wonder he'd heard nothing. There was no room to turn that deep in, so he crawled on his knees and elbows, the flare sizzling a few inches from the tip of his nose. Being that close to it was throwing sunspots into his vision, which activated monster nerves in his imagination.

The tunnel opened enough for him to squeeze around without risking the flare. The sizzling sound had overcast the chittering. The chittering was much, much closer. George stopped a moment, holding his breath, before acting as if his exhalation was the shot from a starter's pistol. He sprint-crawled. He couldn't be cornered, he had to get to the chamber and pick the right tunnel, somehow.

He reached the chamber and the light from the flare cast glow into the tunnel pointed back the way he'd come. Shadows were in motion and antennae danced above undefinable heads. He spun, considered his options, and went with the one in the middle.

23

The ranger had gotten drunk two nights in a row after getting home earlier than expected and finding his wife in bed with the next-door neighbor, Gillian. For about two minutes he thought he was about to have more fun than any ten-years-married man ought to. The fantasy crashed hard enough that he had to sit down. What he saw had nothing to do with him, aside from the archaic ceremony they'd arranged and the silly piece of paper they'd signed with a guy everybody called Pastor Pete.

He was now part of a onesome, not a threesome.

When he awoke, red-eyed and annoyed, he sat up on the ranger station couch—a sturdy, ancient piece of furniture done in a thick cotton polyester blend—and looked out the window. Staring directly back at him were the huge obsidian eyes of a moose. At first, he wondered why a moose would traverse the winding steps of the ranger station—it was more than thirty years old and had long been below the last forestry cut and plant procedure. The elder trees in the forest, and there were many, stood another 160 feet beyond the roof of the ranger's station.

The ranger blinked himself a little more awake.

He wasn't looking at moose eyes, but at a moose eye. It had to be big as a wok. He sat up straight and sucked a deep and excited breath. This moose had to stand twenty-five, thirty feet high, without counting its rack.

The excitement became terror. The moose leaned its head and its great rack against the railing surrounding the ranger station's deck. The fuzzy points of the rack punched through the spruce walls. Other points smashed the big window and sent glass shards out like the shine from a disco ball. The ranger rolled from the couch. In socked feet, he ran to the bedroom and slammed the door. He shot a look out the window and discovered two more moose, calves, but bigger than the biggest moose he'd seen before a minute ago.

The strange notion that he'd shrunk hit him so hard he believed it. He crawled out the small window as the station rocked and began to teeter. Climbing down was no longer an option and he leapt backward, hoping to catch a tree as the station crumbled beneath him in a crashing smash of wood, steel, and plaster.

He didn't.

He broke both legs and dislocated his hip. The ranger clenched his teeth to keep from screaming. If any of these moose saw him…well, who knew what they might do.

The moose paraded in a gleeful show of accomplishment at knocking down the building. They pounced and stamped the ranger station. Bits of the modern world scattered, and the ranger saw his cellphone lying upon a pink pillow of fiberglass insulation. The screen had been shattered, but that was by design, so Apple could sell new screens and employee geeks with little screwdrivers had steady work. The phone would likely still function to some degree.

Everything below the waist was useless, but the ranger was fit and able. He weighed only 170 pounds and a bragworthy sum of that was upper body strength. He reached into the slightly overgrown grass and began pulling himself. He fought the pain and terror, and kept his sounds down to a steady groan. The sweat of agony oozed from his pores, mingling with the whiskey sweats from the nights preceding.

Right there. The phone was right there.

He reached, stretching in a way that seemed to re-snap all the bones he'd broken. His hand fell onto the phone, and he reeled it back. He pressed a button on the side and light played through the fog of broken glass. He attempted to use the touchscreen, but no dice. Three fresh cuts bloomed on his index finger as he swiped. He glanced up at the giant moose. They'd calmed some, standing over the victorious heap of the ranger's station.

The ranger pressed a button and said, "Siri." The command didn't take, so he raised his voice, "Siri—"

The adult moose leapt, bringing its hooves down onto the ranger, silencing his request before he had the chance to make it. Within minutes, the grey larva would sprout from the forest floor and begin to devour the ranger. His phone remained lifeless and dark until it began to ring two days later when Mandy Ng tried to reach him from the hotel, about an hour after she set out on a rescue mission.

24

"...and this spot right here is where James South and Garth Crenshaw blew themselves and the space gator to smithereens," the tour guide said, eyes shining, gazing off into the wide-open space where the grand visit from beyond Earth's solar system came to its exciting conclusion. "The flames lit in an incredible ball and every survivor in town heard the bang, many had been looking to the sky for answers and saw the fantastic light show."

Nobody in town had seen the mostly lightless explosion, and only a few who had been outside already had heard the bang. The tour group didn't question it. They'd come from all over to visit the island and the tours had been packed from the first day they'd begun taking people around.

The group now milled about the rather drab patch of land. A handful filled jars and small containers with dirt, unaware that between the steady rains and what everyone assumed was a military presence had combed the land, that there wouldn't be much more than a particle of gator debris in those samples. Still, it was a memento. The tour wasn't currently equipped to create souvenirs and thusly couldn't begrudge these small thefts from the land.

The guide was about to suggest that they hop back into the vans, as the rain was really starting to come down, but a group of non-English speaking tourists began running and shouting. The rest of the group paused, scanning for the disturbance.

The space was wide-open but surrounded on three sides by thick bush. Fir trees mostly, rising well over forty feet. From the shadows, a massive face appeared, big as a Nissan Micra. The tour guide blinked and tried to make sense of it.

A cougar.

It leapt from the trees, soaring over the van and all those standing still, to the small group that had spotted the beast first. It slammed two and then pounced on the others, like a housecat. The rest of the group began to run in a chaotic scattering.

"Get in the van!" the guide shouted.

One young man stood almost still, his phone out, camera on his face while over his shoulder the enormous mountain lion pounced on tourists. Content, baby.

Seven tourists ran to one van and two to the other. The guide ran to the closest van—the one with only two passengers—and started the engine. Somewhere, mauled and unable to move, was the second guide with the keys in her pocket. Van in gear, the guide rolled.

The tourists who'd picked the wrong van streamed out and the beast pounced, slamming paws like a wide-eyed puppy to a treefrog in the grass. People were screaming and crying. The cougar bit and shook, flung people, pawed at them, as if trying to keep the game alive despite being declared the winner in a unanimous decision.

The guide looked anywhere but at the mirrors. She wasn't about to slow down for anyone or anything. The wipers screeched and she turned up the volume on the stereo. The island didn't have the typical emergency services available, so for a lack of a better option, her new plan was to get to the pier, tell someone with a modicum of authority, and hope like hell that the ferry was docked and ready to depart.

"You're leaving them?" said a man from the backseat of the van.

The guide didn't answer, focused instead on the road and steadily worsening storm.

25

Along the western shore, a colony of sixteen seals lazed on the beach, bloated and sickly. Freshwater from the island played into the ocean steadily near where they lay. The seals had retreated from the waters in fear that they'd be next.

It had begun a week ago, by human standards. Four seals, larger than the largest walruses, disappeared one at a time, eaten by still larger predators. One of the predators was pregnant. An orca a team of government scientists were monitoring and had named Judy, was suddenly not doing well. She could hardly move. The baby inside her grew and grew and grew until bursting its mother, sending out a rain of pink debris. The baby snapped up the meat and then began chasing after seals and walruses alike. It devoured the delicious meat at a pace that spooked the entire oceanic eco-system. Within five days, the baby had grown to the size of a blue whale and wasn't through getting bigger.

With the local aquatic life in hiding, and the 35-foot orca being ignorant to killer whale traits, the creature went haywire with hunger. It launched itself onto the beach, snatching the thrashing and helpless seals.

They learned and scooched further from the water. The massive orca began patrolling, its nature ideals on game going out the window. It looked to bigger fish, the biggest fish—a strangely loud and incredibly large fish, one with fins that spun instead of flapping—and decided that if it came back, it was going to attack, no matter the length and bulk differences.

26

Mandy found the number for BC Ferries and spoke to a woman named Mona. Mona explained that one of the local tour guides and two of her guests had pulled in talking the same stuff about an emergency and very large animals.

"It's not like what you think. These animals are monstrous. Coyotes like those little two-seater cars. Incredible," Mandy said.

"Oh, so…?"

"So, tell them on the far side to send the ship over empty and that'll it'll be full to capacity on the way home." A thought struck Mandy like a shovel to the back of the head. "Christ, there must be a hundred campers in the park."

"You mean like actually big, like how the space gator was?" Mona said.

"That's it. Call them and tell them."

Mandy hung up and swung open the center drawer of the check-in desk. She pulled out a small black book. Jacy was in her kitchen whites and had been doing a lot of nothing for the last two hours on account that nobody had been served food; she came over and looked askance of Mandy.

Mandy dialed the ranger station's number. "There's huge beasts. More of them," she said to

Jacy as the line rang and rang and rang. She hung up the phone and ran a finger along the book.

"What do you mean? Like more gators? How can there be more gators? Oh my god!" Jacy said.

"Not gators," Mandy said.

She had the phone pressed to her ear. She looked up and then dialed Roger Gordon's cellphone—he was the park ranger on this month. He'd been in the hotel the night before, drunk and rambling about his wife turning gay.

"What then?" Jacy said.

A few would-be patrons of the restaurant had gathered around Jacy.

"Coyotes, slugs, deer, maybe everything," Mandy said, only answering Jacy because nobody was answering the phone.

"In the forest?" Jacy said. "George is in the forest, with a reporter!"

Mandy slammed the phone into its cradle. "George? He came back?" She ran a finger down the list of numbers before flipping to the next page and starting over.

Through the main doors, dripping with rainwater, came the fishermen who'd rescued Denver and failed to rescue Ilya. The big man with the little head said, "We took him to the terminal. His wound is dressed and there's a doctor who happened to be catching the next ferry out. Says the guy will be okay."

Mandy nodded. "Anybody down there talking about giant animals?" She found the number she sought and began punching it into the phone.

"Yeah. There was a woman who'd been

camping—at the base diamond, not the park—and she said there was a rat as big as a dog."

Mandy put up a finger. "Chuck? It's Mandy. There's been animal attacks and we need to clear out the island. You have the keys to the town bunker?" She waited a moment, listening. "You think the old air raid siren works?"

It had been installed during WWII, in case the Japanese decided to invade.

The hotel lobby held its collective breath. All were waiting for word on what was happening and what needed to be done. Nobody noticed that Jacy had run off.

27

Lin got to about ten feet from the Honda and stopped. The windshield had been smashed out and the hood now featured a crater-like dent that worked its way to an inch from each side. Whatever had hit the hood was undeniably heavy. She recommenced moving forward, though much more slowly. Playing cautious had to be done, but what about the dangers lurking behind her?

She cracked some, a single harried sob playing up from her chest. She closed her eyes and saw not only June's face, but all the kids' faces, and Devon's face, and what about a fifth? If she survived, she could probably slide a fifth face into the image, sixth if her own was there too. And it would have to be. She wasn't about to surrender to this island, wasn't about to allow the universe to play it otherwise.

A fresh new possibility popped to mind as she rounded the passenger's side of the Honda: what if George's desiccated body was lying on the ground at the back, or maybe he was dead in the trunk. What if an animal was feeding on his corpse right now?

"Don't be dead," she said.

George wouldn't have been up here if it wasn't for her…though he would've been on the island anyway. The natural compulsion to circumnavigate guilt had her closing her eyes, unwilling to see what might be there.

She rounded the back and took a deep breath before opening her eyes and looking into the yawning hatch.

Empty.

"Huh," she said and pulled the hatch closed. "George, are you out here?"

She waited a moment.

"George?"

A rustling came from a patch of bushes, and she didn't wait to see the culprit. She was in the Honda and backing out in a matter of a handful of seconds. Turned around, she saw it then. A frog. Like the spider, like the snake, this thing was nightmare-fuel massive.

She gunned the gas pedal and the frog leapt at her. It nailed the window and the tip of the pink tongue pressed through the shattered glass, its blood spurting a cool shot onto Lin's cheek before the frog fell away, taking the broken glass with it.

"What in the hell is this place?" she said.

She had to slow down. The road was winding and slim. The rains were getting heavy and without a windshield, she was squinting against the spray. Part of the road further down had washed out some in a low spot around a curve and she slowed to single digits in extreme caution.

From the corner of her eye, she saw a pack of huge rats feasting on what appeared to be a wolf. The wolf was as big as a skinny cow, its fur thinned and matted.

"How are you possible?" Lin said.

She had an impulse to snap a shot, and then recalled her cellphone. She opened the center console and snatched it up from the charger pad. The little bars in the upper right corner were gone and the symbol for emergencies only reigned.

"How does this island even exist?"

She looked away from her phone when she felt the thumping of mud and then the swish of long grass beneath her undercarriage. She yanked the wheel to resume following the road. Her tires dug into mud and the Honda tilted, skidding against the turn, sliding closer and closer to a ditch. The all-wheel safety system engaged, and the driver's side took over and the engine revved without putting much power to the axles. She popped and thumped over the ridge of the shoulder and was back on the road. The engine engaged the axles fully and she jerked forward.

Town was just ahead. She scooped her phone from the center console again and flipped through her contacts. In the middle of a dead street—feeling safe on asphalt—she dialed home.

28

George had been scared all along, but now he was truly terrified. The flare was sputtering. He had been crouch-walking for an indeterminate amount of time. The tunnel was by far the longest yet. All the while the chittering sounds were growing in nearness and locations. They seemed to be coming from everywhere—though still most predominately coming from behind. Whatever was down there with him, it wasn't alone.

For once, he tried to think of anything but comic book monsters. There were scores of what ifs and possible creatures. He wanted nothing to do with any of them. In fact, he attempted to summon silly things, like a team of ladybugs, maybe a little large but just as harmless as ever. Or perhaps the tunnels weren't built by bugs at all, maybe there were a few bugs chirping into an echo chamber that simply continued bouncing forever and these tunnels were old pirate treasure tunnels. He'd watched tons of episodes of that Oak Island show, maybe they were on the wrong island, on the wrong coast. What if he stumbled onto doubloons and holy relics?

Yeah, right.

His head brushed the top of the tunnels and dirt cascaded down his face and into his mouth. He spat. He moaned. He fought to keep from breaking down. If there was ever a time to be a man, this was it.

His back was beginning to ache. Pushing through the aggravation, he bent himself a little lower yet. He had to promise himself that at the end of this tunnel was freedom, and that it was no big deal if the flare went out.

And even if it did, it's not as if he could go but two ways.

No, it wouldn't be a big deal if it went out.

Not. At. All.

The flare sputtered in his hand, and he held his breath, as if he might accidentally blow it out like a friend's birthday candle. He could lie to himself all he liked, but if he didn't escape before the flare died, he might crumble internally.

He took a deep, solidifying breath and hurried on. For a few moments there, fogged by the highs and lows of possibilities, he'd lost track of the chittering. It was so close behind him. It was through the walls on either side, and though it was more distant, it was also coming from in front of him.

His head bumped again as the tunnel shrank another few inches. His back sang the song of trouble but was only whispering the lyrics yet. The flare remained steady, even as he switched arms. His hands got sweaty quickly and his forearms got hot.

He took three more crouched steps and discovered his head dragging against the ceiling anew. He dropped gently to his knees. Tears had begun to spill. He couldn't help it. They mingled with the dry soil and streaked mud down his cheeks. He nearly cried out for his mother, but she was dead. As was his father. As was his Uncle Shane. As was Carole's mom, Josie. Carole was in no shape and some other woman was to come. When would it stop? When did he get to be a kid again? When would the world let him think only about video games and math tests and girls?

Jacy.

He could cry out for Jacy and she was maybe close enough to hear him, yet infinite miles away. He was alone and the tunnel kept shrinking.

"You can hear them ahead," he whispered, egging himself onward, away from the thought that this tunnel dead-ended and the chittering things were coming up behind him. Cornering him.

He pushed onward, his chin's quiver the only fast motion he could muster. He closed his eyes a moment and imagined a door. He imagined crawling through the door and discovering the Picture House Lodge parking lot. Jacy would be there. She'd hug him and kiss him. Somebody would give a damn about him.

He opened his eyes, hardened to the world, certain he could keep going. The tunnel would run until a door appeared and he'd survive this as he'd survived so much else. Luck was his friend; it had been his friend even when it destroyed those around him. Luck was—

The flare spat three mini-firework bursts before it went out. George was plunged into complete dark, and the chittering sounds were coming from everywhere. They seemed only slightly lesser from in front. He'd cornered himself.

Terrified, he began shuffling faster. He could, too, now that he had two free hands. On and on he rushed and smaller and smaller the tunnel became. His shoulders brushed at his sides as he swallowed down a sobbing moan.

Perhaps his mother could help him, after the things caught up to him, after they feasted upon his flesh and cleaned his bones. She could help him get acquainted with whatever happened once a body bit the big one.

29

Miriam had left Lucy's store with a couple t-shirts and a couple DVDs about two hours earlier and then had returned to her hotel room to lie down. When she awoke, she headed downstairs for coffee and watched from the edge of the lobby as people scurried around.

"What's happened?" she said to a young white man in a hemp poncho, hair in matted dreadlocks.

"The monster, dude, it came back or something," he said.

Miriam frowned and stepped to the only occupied chair in the lobby. An old man in a flannel shirt leaned forward, a hand on a cane that was carved and lacquered, and was decorated with feathers that dangled from a leather tie.

"What's happened?" she said.

The man sucked at his gums as he side-eyed Miriam. "Looks like we're going to be hunkering down again."

"Why?"

"The island's gone foul. Big bugs, big animals, big trouble."

Miriam straightened and watched the disorganized dance of chaos. She had to make a call. "Thanks," she said before hurrying back up to her room for some quiet. In the second-floor hallway she passed a woman with three sleepy-looking children. "You might want to lay low a while, something's going on."

The woman tilted her head before replying in a string of German.

Miriam tossed her hands up and continued along the unfinished hallway. The contractors Mandy had hired worked wonders at getting the rooms back to rentable, though not really presentable. Miriam opened her door and let it wheeze closed behind her. From her pocket came her phone. She scrolled through her contacts until she arrived at the name RICHTER COHAGEN. She had to take a pause for a moment, just having this man's contact sent butterflies into her guts. It was like having Bezos' number or Musk's number or Jack Ma's number—before the Chinese government kidnapped him and appropriated his wealth. Her thumb trembled but came down on the number the same as if it had been steady.

She listened as the line rang and rang and rang. Finally, the man himself picked up. He was so, so famous that his voice was unmistakable.

"Miriam Weever, how can I help you?"

"Uh, hi, Mr. Cohagen. There's something going on, like you said would probably happen…well, not exactly like you said…it's—"

"Giganticized animalia?" Richter Cohagen said, a little bit of his Baltic accent shining through with his smile.

"You knew this would happen?" Miriam forgot her awe of the man a moment, her mind replacing it was awe for the man's disregard for human life.

"I'd hoped. I have a few men installed and watching things. What I need you to do is gather up all the information on every homeowner. The government will be deeming Picture Island unliveable in the next few days, and I will come in with fair offers to all the residents, with you acting as proxy. Nobody can know it's me, not yet."

Miriam shook her head in five quick jerks. There was nothing she could do to stop this now, might as well get paid in the process. "All right. I'll do that…you know, so long as I don't get eaten or squashed or something."

"Stay in your room. I'll have someone come escort you where you need to go to gather all the information not available online. The residents there, it's like the Dark Ages."

"Okay."

There were a handful of weighty, silent seconds.

"And Miriam?"

"Yeah?"

"I'm impressed. Keep up the good work…don't drink the water."

The line went dead in her ear. She couldn't help but be proud that this billionaire complimented her, despite that he—and his entire ilk—were comic book level egomaniacal and wholly disdainful of life below their economic class.

30

Lin wiped her eyes. She'd just now gotten off the phone with Devon. He gave her the next ferry sailing time, as well as giving her the number for the local water taxi service. The worst of it was behind her and now all she had to do was ride the boat the hell out of there and pick up the pieces in the coming days, weeks, months, years—it might be forever, she might never recover from the trauma of what she'd survived.

Once she had her wits enough, she dialed the water taxi's number. It immediately went to voicemail: "We're fully booked through tonight and tomorrow. We apologize for any inconvenience. If you'd like to book a time for after that, please leave a message and someone will get back to you ASAP." A buzzy ping sounded and she hung up. It occurred to her that she was maybe far from alone in her tribulations. Perhaps George had made it down from the forest and had told everyone what he'd seen.

She did a quick lookup of the BC Ferries numbers and dialed the one associated with Picture Island. Someone answered this time.

"BC Ferries, Picture Island."

"Can I reserve a spot on the next ferry?"

The woman on the line huffed once. "No.

We're overloading, and we'll never get everyone on. One woman told me she saw rats bigger than her border collie and a man told me he saw a wild turkey big enough to serve *him* for Thanksgiving."

"Oh."

"Get here whenever. Won't make any difference, no way you get on the first sailing. God help us if the weather gets any worse."

"Oh."

"Yeah. Good luck."

The line clicked off and Lin looked at her phone screen. She decided she'd try the number she had for George. It didn't ring and went to a Bell telephone automated message.

"Shit," she said, coming to terms yet again that she might have gotten a child killed. But what could she do about it now? She glanced to her rear-view mirror. She could go back up there and look for him. "Damn."

The seconds became minutes as rain showered through the broken windshield. She was already sopping, and now hardly noticed the increase. Not even an hour ago she was hanging upside down in a tree, awaiting her demise by spider exsanguination. Jesus.

She scratched the side of her head and the damp cigarette fell to her lap. It wasn't about to get any drier. She put it between her lips and reached into her pocket for the torch lighter. It took seventeen pushes to the igniter paddle before a weak flame sputtered.

She spoke around an exhalation. "That's lucky."

As the cigarette sizzled through the halfway point, Lin watched the street. Worms like pythons began to poke up through the dirt before sliding back down and hiding away. The magnifying effect of their enlargement made the texture of them all the more revolting. She shivered. The greasy ridges and the slink and stretch of their motions was something out of this world.

"It's as if they came from…" she trailed.

Walking quickly up the street in cook's whites was a girl. She carried a junior-sized Sher-Wood hockey stick. She was dripping wet, but set on going wherever she was going, which appeared to be up the hill and into the forest.

"I wouldn't go up there," Lin called out the glassless window of the driver's door.

The girl paused and then squinted. "How come? I've been up there before. My friend George is up there, I think. Nobody is going to check, and he isn't answering my texts."

The words came out in a lightning rumble of high-pitched syllables. Lin unpacked it all and then caught up.

"You're Jacy Popper," she said.

The girl straightened. "Yeah, so what?"

The boat would get there soon enough, but she wouldn't be on the first sailing…and she owed George some consideration. That he hadn't gone to find his girlfriend suggested he was still out there, though now assumedly dead.

"Look, there's big bugs up there. We'll need more than a hockey stick. You tell me where we can find some weaponry and I'll take you up the hill."

Jacy stepped closer. "You're the reporter woman? The one who caught George and was making him take the ferry back so he could go live with some woman he never even met?"

Lin nodded. "It would make more sense if you looked at it from an adult's perspective." She paused a moment. "Look, you can't go up on foot. A spider had me and I got lucky. I guess George ran away."

Jacy shook her head. "George wouldn't leave you behind unless he couldn't help it."

"If we find him, we can ask," Lin said, thinking, *if he's even alive.* "But first, we need better arms. Any ideas?"

Jacy pushed her mouth to the left side of her face. "Umm, maybe my uncle has stuff. He texted me and said to meet them at the terminal, so I know nobody's home."

"Get in."

"He has this thing called a Gator. It has six wheels and can go just about anywhere but underwater. We should take that to check the trails. My uncle took me on it once, it's like a slow dune buggy."

Lin shrugged. It would hardly make a difference now if she put any additional damage on her Honda, but then again, it wasn't exactly trail ready.

31

The tunnel had become so tight around George that he had to use his elbows, dragging his pelvis as he shimmied a clumsy breaststroke over the dirt. The chittering was catching up to him. The walls around him seemed to thin and the only thing that didn't change much was that the quietest target was still straight ahead of him.

Dirt rained steady over his shoulders and neck, little balls of it rolling down the collar of his shirt and a few skirting his waistband to end up in his underwear. He felt dirty all over. At least the tears had dried up. As if to make up for the moisture, now and then drips fell through the ceiling or he'd sink a body part into an unseen puddle. The tunnels seemed a whole lot less sturdy in these moments.

"Just a little further," he whispered.

He felt dirt spray out at him from his left. He paused, terrified and curious. The chittering grew hugely loud after a moment and another burst of dirt. George got it then: the things were putting two tunnels into one and were so, so much closer than he ever imagined.

His body went into overdrive, and he shuffled like a soldier crossing no man's land. A steady whine played from his mouth. Behind him, the chittering grew louder. He felt the vibrations of their digging play through him, rumbling his core like war drum strikes. There was zero doubt that if they caught him, they'd kill him. Law of the jungle.

From his right, he felt a dirt spray, and the chittering chorus grew louder. He didn't slow this time, even with the tunnel shrinking by another six inches. The insectile cacophony had him on the verge of covering his head and letting the things kill him. At least it would be over then and he'd feel no more of this terror. The dread of knowing they'd get him had to be worse than the few moments from the time they got him to the time they finished him.

And still, he shuffled forward as fast as he could, unwilling to brave out the moment, unwilling to snuff out the glimmer of hope staying alive carried for him. Being a kid, death had never been real in the sense that it might happen to him, even when so many died around him, and then he came to Picture Island and the place wanted to eat him alive. Perhaps if he let it, everything would settle.

The steady moan grew louder, but it didn't matter. The chittering things were so, so close now and—

His forehead struck a wall as his elbows sunk into mud. The tunnel dead-ended—such a befitting term. The chittering sounds were on him and he felt the first stiff jabs of the things' feet touching his calves and ankles.

"No!" he screamed and began clawing at the dirt before him, tossing big handfuls behind him as he wriggled, shrinking himself for protection against the chittering things behind him.

They were on him. They weighed little, but were hard and frantic, clawing at his flesh, scratching scores into everything they touched while tearing his clothes.

"Git!" he screeched, digging, digging, digging.

Water droplets began to rain down on him. He had to be close to the surface, but he could dig no longer. He spun, reaching down and taking the front legs of the hard thing. It chittered maniacally and he lashed his arms outward while still gripping the boney limbs as far as they'd go. One leg snapped free. He began beating against the thing. More legs scrambled against him. Great mandibles pressed the flesh of his face, pinning him as it tried for an angle that would allow it to take its meal.

George struggled and jerked and pushed the thing hard against the ceiling. Dirt began raining down over him quicker than before and he had to close his eyes and his mouth, had to hold his breath or be drowned in dirt. The chittering became extreme, more frantic. George felt the flesh of his throat begin to burn. Scratched? Cut? There was no way to know for sure and no time to check. He continued twisting and smashing. A second leg came off in his hand and for a moment, he imagined winning this battle.

Fresh new mandibles attacked his feet. A second thing. He jerked and squirmed, wrenching and pulling. Finally, the first thing's shell snapped, and cool fluid cascaded over him. He couldn't help but attempt a scream, letting go all the precious oxygen he had left. The fluid and the dirt filled his mouth. A fresh new panic streamed into his muscles, and he flopped and kicked and punched his arms over his head. His lungs screamed where his mouth couldn't.

A fresh weight clumped down on him, different from the loose dirt. He heard a new sound: an animal growling. Water poured over him and he began to slide. Light filled the world around him and he gasped once. The dirt in his eyes stung terribly, but he had to look. He didn't see any animals, but he did see two-dozen beetles the size of small dogs, and a few bigger. All were black with long antennae, horrible mandibles, and spindly legs. These were the creators of the tunnel and the masters of his current terror.

He moaned, "Mommy," under his breath.

The things, all of them, including ones in freshly caved-in tunnels he hadn't yet spotted, came for him. He was invading their space, a trespasser, an interloper, a target for their wrath. He tried to roll onto his knees but discovered his adrenaline had been spent. Running on fumes, he tried to ball in tight, even as the first of the things jabbed at him.

The chittering was so fantastic, he didn't hear that growl, though it was much closer now.

32

The ferry blew its airhorn. People had piled in by car and by foot. The parking decks were loaded and the seating capacity was full. No more than ninety vehicles and three hundred people could be seated on the ferry. The capacity rules weren't just for fun. The ferry could handle only so much, and with the storm as it was, the crossing would take three times as long.

Denver was on and coming to from the first bout of drugs he'd been served. He was missing a foot, but he was alive. It was the general consensus amid the crowd as they talked about what they'd seen and heard. Things that could've killed them but didn't, so they had to be relieved, even thankful that the universe gave them the opportunity for tomorrows.

BC Ferries had some forethought none of them on the island had considered, and though it left a smaller headcount for passengers, they'd sent along twenty extra heads to help with security. They weren't police, or even trained guards, they appeared to be the sum of all the men, as well as a couple biggish women, who worked for the company and lived in the small towns around the pier on the mainland. When people got a little rough with each other, a figure in a reflective vest stepped in. In a modern world, where office jobs were the norm, people who did anything physical for work typically loomed large enough to quell poor behavior.

Mandy watched from the pier, her rifle against her shoulder. A huge crash sounded further inland of the docks. All those not being shut away by the close maw of the big ship turned their heads—many on the ship were looking and shouting, but the rumble of the ferry's great engine devoured their warnings.

A 25-, 30-foot moose loomed over the largest building, stomping and kicking as it looked around frantically. Car alarms cried out and glass shattered.

"My house!" shouted someone from the crowd.

The moose had the frantic eyes of a housecat during the witching hour. It lowered its great rack and bolted straight for the main drag, which featured a block of two-story buildings: businesses below and apartments above. The moose raked its incredible rack through the storefronts.

"Sonofabitch!" Lucy said. She was in the loose group, was wearing one of the new batch of I SURVIVED THE SPACE GATOR ATTACK ON PICTURE ISLAND t-shirts. "That was my store!"

The moose finally looked at the people. It paused a moment.

From the east again, came the crash and bang of two smaller moose. Neither had racks, but it didn't seem to matter. They took to mimicking the larger moose, stomping and headbutting.

"Mandy, help bring everyone this way."

Mandy turned to face Miriam the realtor. "Huh?" Mandy said, hands tight on her long, long rifle.

The biggest moose started toward them, slowly. It stomped on Jimmy Jackson's fully restored Yugo and a voice in the crowd whined, "Aww, man."

"The, uh, new owner of the fish warehouse says we can hide in the basement," Miriam said. "Come on, help me get everyone inside!"

"New owner?" Mandy finally looked away from the big moose and to Miriam. She was already ten feet away and chasing behind a man built like an action figure. Many others chased and Mandy started waving her arms as if herding cattle. "Come on, let's go! We can stay put until the ferry comes back!"

The lingering crowd began peeling their eyes from the moose and moving in the smart direction. One man ran against the stream, toward Mandy.

Roy Popper grabbed onto Mandy and said, "Where's Jacy?"

Mandy didn't know, hadn't considered the girl left in her charge, and said, "Must be in the warehouse already. Go!"

All three moose began jogging after the crowd. Mandy brought up the rear like she was the caboose. The beasts were gaining quickly. Roy took a hard right through the door of the warehouse, Mandy five feet behind him. Mandy took that same hard right then, feeling the vibration of the closing footfalls. Roy burned after the last man chasing down the concrete stairs. Mandy was hot behind him. The clang and crunch that filled the air made Mandy jump at the head of the stairs and she rolled, never losing grip on her rifle, even as the steel warehouse lifted and flopped off the foundation as if plucked away by a tornado.

The smaller moose quickly joined in after the larger moose, but everyone was beneath the reenforced floor—designed to withstand thousands of pounds of fish, equipment, and delivery vehicles. It was dark down there and everyone crowded to the eastern wall. The western side opened to the water and was where, when active, they not-so-secretly dumped unwanted and rotting catch.

"Jacy? Jacy?" Roy shouted.

Nobody else spoke, only little moans and the occasional squeak of terror exited their lips. There were two windows high up on walls and those closest watched the scene in muted fascination until one of them said, "Oh, no. There's people."

"Is it Jacy?" Ruby Popper said.

Roy pushed through the crowd and stepped up on a bench to see out the window better. "That's my gator!" he said.

A handful freaked out and began screaming. The rest were locals and knew his Gator was the six-wheeled, John Deere UTV he hadn't shut up about since buying it three years ago.

"Look at that kitty!" someone yelled.

Mandy did quick math and barged through the crowd and to the window. She brought up her rifle and aimed, waiting, waiting, waiting for the animal to still so that she might nail it—though into an animal that big, it wasn't likely to do much more than irritate it, and hopefully confuse it a little.

33

Lin drove the Gator up the hill. Jacy had wanted to take the wheel, but Lin had said no, Jacy had to be happy being the gunner and holding the .22 with an extended magazine, currently loaded with birdshot. The birdshot, though far less deadly, was helpful because Jacy was aiming from a moving vehicle. Two frogs had taken shrapnel after missed shots struck nearby rocks.

Once up the hill, they followed what appeared to be a semi-fresh footpath down the hill behind Josie's demolished home. Lin white-knuckled it down the other side, picking up way more speed than she was comfortable with. They drove the Gator into the creek, soaking them to their knees and disturbing a fish big enough to stuff and be the prized possession of an entire trailer park.

Lin yanked hard right to get out of the creek, but Jacy reached over and pushed the wheel away from the embankment. A cavern had formed only a few feet onto the shore and stretched out almost ten feet in length.

"Think he fell in?" Lin said after braking.

Jacy hopped off the Gator and hurried to the edge. Down there, in the soft dirt were sneaker prints.

"I think—"

Jacy's words were silenced by the ground

crumbling beneath her. She had to jump back. The creek began dumping into the hole and following it downhill.

"We need to keep going down." Jacy got up, dripping, the water all up her back to the bottom of her long bob hairdo. "I saw his shoe marks!"

"Okay. Okay," Lin said and on they went.

The creek became shallower with every foot, the flowing water outpacing them. Fish and overlarge bugs raced to keep pace. It was all so incredible that it had become mundane. Obviously everything on Picture Island was massive and monstrous and reshuffling the deck that had once put humans near the top of the food chain game.

"It's all caving! Look!" Jacy shouted over the growl of the Gator engine—it clearly preferred a drier running experience.

Just on the shore, a path crumbled in, and massive beetles squirmed and danced in panic. Jacy took pointless shots at their big, black backs. The island was falling apart. Nothing was set up for animals and insects of this magnitude, nature wasn't coping.

"Stop!" Jacy shouted.

The gush of water had met a lip and slowed for the moment down in the tunnels. Many beetles floated on their backs, but something else floated in with them. An eight-inch plastic tube. Red. Lin had explained to Jacy in colorful detail—as was Lin's way when relaying a story—about how she'd sent George to get the emergency kit from her vehicle, and everything within that kit. Including flares. Had George thought to take flares with him? They did that in movies and comics all the time. George survived on knowing what everyday people did to become heroes in stories.

"Is that a flare?" Jacy shouted.

Between the growling engine and the steady downpour and the creek gushing into the beetles' tunnels, her voice was barely a blip.

"What?"

"Is that a flare!"

Lin had her eyes on Jacy's lips as they moved and then leaned over the seat to look. "Yes!"

The wall of dirt that had created a lip within the tunnel disappeared and the heavy flow gushed unimpeded down a new path, taking the dead beetles and the spent flare with it.

"Go!" Jacy said.

Lin hit the gas pedal and they hurried on downward, following the hill, back toward town. They veered and skidded and nearly rolled twice. They weren't far from the road. The creek bed had disappeared from beneath them and they began cutting through grass and occasionally had to skirt a patch of youngling trees. The tunnels remained with them, guiding them to the end goal.

"Holy shit!" Jacy said and aimed the rifle.

34

Water gushed heavily around George, and he felt himself lifted from the mud. The beetles at his feet were no longer jabbing him, they now seemed instead to be clinging to him, using him as a life raft. Another latched onto his left arm. One latched onto his side. Quickly, he wore a suit of beetles as he floated with the rush over water.

At least he could breathe.

A fresh panic took over, imagining what would happen if they got to dry shore together, and he tried to free himself from the clutches of the beetles. They clung tight as June bugs to a screen door. Something stopped him and the water pounded hard against his chest and face. Pop sounds rang out and something clipped his ear so hard it dulled all other pain. He couldn't breathe again. He inhaled the gushing flow. The beetles lost their grips.

Something let behind him and the wall disappeared. He heard more pops and that animalistic growling as he tumbled amid the wash of water and bug parts. His right ear was screaming in pain, but if he'd been tired before, he was done now. Exhaustion wasn't a big enough word, didn't encompass how drained he felt physically while his mind raced. As he lay, a fresh new sting stabbed into his shoulder, a moment before he heard the echoing pop.

"Stop shooting!"

The two beetles clinging to his legs pressed into him and distantly through a fog he saw humanoid shapes. They were beating on the beetles. Hands came down on him.

"George! George!"

His mind clicked. That was Jacy Popper. His girlfriend.

George couldn't see her, not really, but she loomed over him in the most angelic shape in the history of angelic shapes.

35

"Hurry! Hurry!" Lin said.

She and Jacy had gathered up a battered—and accidentally birdshot—George and were loading him into the dumper bed at the back of the Gator. The tunnels had washed through the side of the hill and onto the asphalt of a street that, in less than a block away, crossed with the road that led to the hot springs.

That George had bugs on him was awful. That there were so many bugs at all was worse. Neither of these facts mattered much in the face of a reality that included a cougar as big as a monster truck loping in their direction from north of town, following the road.

"I thought cats didn't like water," Jacy said as she popped into the shotgun seat, arm draped into the back, holding hands with a barely conscious George.

"Big cats ain't afraid of a little water," Lin said.

As a new reporter she'd done a fluff piece—her editor had said, 'get it, fluff piece?' and she'd just had to smile and nod—on a litter of desert lynx housecats this woman had trained to swim in the pond in her backyard. Lin had been instructed to present this as something fascinating, but the keeper of these animals had pointed out that most wild cats weren't quite as *pussy* as housecats. Lin rambled this story as she wheeled the achingly slow Gator toward the hotel.

Jacy got wide eyed. "Two puns in one! My dad loves puns. He says—!"

Lin had to swerve around a rat that popped up in their path, hard enough to silence Jacy for a moment, almost losing her and George in the process. But that rat looked big enough to bite off a human leg from the knee down in a single chomp. Also, big enough to tip the UTV. It chased after them a moment, though seemed to think better of it. The cougar was hot on their trail.

It leapt. The paws missed smashing them, though managed to knock them sideways. Lin jerked to hold the wheel and keep them steady as she rolled them into the parking lot at the side of the hotel. The left wheels of the Gator rose and continued rising until the machine was flipping and the occupants were spilled onto the asphalt.

Lin had conked her head, and was seeing stars, and the rest of the marshmallow shapes in a bowl of Lucky Charms. A primal need pushed her to her hands and knees. She glanced to her right and there was Jacy, up and dragging George, the resiliency of youth keeping her moving.

"It's coming!" Jacy screeched and Lin looked over her shoulder as she pushed to her feet.

The cougar reared back its right paw, claws out and big enough to slash her head from her neck without much consideration on aim. Lin closed her eyes and imagined her family without her. The paw hit her, though with little force—still enough to send her to her ass. She blinked up at the fantastic lion as it scanned the world around it, lowered to its haunches, ready to fight whatever it was that had thwarted its effort at an easy kill.

Lin crawled after Jacy who continued to drag George out of the rain and into the building. Up to her feet, she stumbled behind Jacy.

"Where we going?" she said.

"The kitchen."

"Why?"

Jacy didn't answer.

36

"Holy shit, you hit it," Ruby Popper said.

"My Gator," Roy moaned.

Mandy shook her head. She'd known these two a long time and they were nothing short of weirdoes. Their entire brood was like that, and she suddenly got why Jacy didn't fit in with them. Originally, she'd thought it was because Jacy talked so much—and that was part of it, sure—but now she saw that these people were a breed unto themselves.

A loud engine buzzed. The group turned to face the open end of the warehouse where pale light streamed in and water splashed over the lip. About a third of all the people awaiting the second ferry were in that basement. Others had hunkered down in homes, cars, and on boats.

Mandy suddenly thought of Chuck. At the southernmost end of town was a small hall, beneath it was a large military bunker. On a post outside was an air raid siren. She sighed; he obviously hadn't gotten there after their brief phone call.

"Hope you made it, if you went," she whispered.

"We can take most of ya," the fisherman with the little head shouted, leaning from about twenty feet into the water, bobbing on the waves.

Through the window to the east, the moose

were honking at each other, almost certainly over the appearance of a predator in their midst. Mandy swallowed. It would be like a damned Godzilla sequel if this foursome went at it. For now, they were keeping their distance.

The fishing boat had sent out two life rafts to collect people. All the tourists hurried to get in line, as did everyone with children. The only people who seemed disinterested were Mandy, Miriam, and the man who'd led them into the basement. He held a bulky tablet with a squat antenna nubbed out at its top. On the screen was a satellite map.

Mandy began to wonder in the comparatively dull moments who had bought the fish warehouse—and when in the hell had it gone up for sale? "Who is he?" she said to Miriam.

"He's help," Miriam said, a pained expression on her face.

"Help? Who bought the warehouse?" Mandy said.

"That's all we can take!" a voice called out from behind them.

Mandy glanced back and saw they were down to thirteen people. Was that lucky or unlucky?

"A client who wants to remain nameless," Miriam said, she wore a pained expression.

Mandy guessed she'd let the secret slip if this musclebound dude posing as a regular tourist—flannel shirt, Wrangler jeans, nondescript boots—wasn't standing there. She addressed him instead of prodding at Miriam. "Hey, who the hell is your boss?" She hadn't consciously meant to but was pointing the barrel of her rifle at the man.

He glanced up. “You want to make it out of this, you’ll point that elsewhere,” he said. Something on his tablet pinged and he tapped a button. “Sir?”

On the screen was Richter Cohagen. Mandy scrunched up her entire face. “What in the fuck?” she said.

“Dillon. The weather is delaying the helicopters. Hunker down, reinforcements will arrive as soon as possible.”

“Yes, sir,” this bulky man, this Dillon said.

The screen went blank.

“Your boss is Richter Cohagen?”

Miriam posted a false grin on her face. “Mandy, have you considered selling Picture House Lodge?”

Before any kind of answer left her lips, the air raid siren began roaring through the small town of Ghost Clearing. The cougar quit sniffing around the lobby doors of the hotel and the moose ceased smashing the town. The thirteen who remained beneath the fish warehouse bunched up tight to the window to look toward the old hall. Chuck wasn’t visible, but a few people ran from nearby houses toward the hall’s entrance.

Dillon’s tablet pinged again. A square head appeared on the screen. “Dillon?”

“Here.” Dillon pointed the tablet to his face.

“Anybody there know about this siren?”

Dillon looked to Miriam. As she explained, the siren wheezed away like its batteries had died. The building appeared fine, though the cougar had meandered closer to it.

37

The sudden noise and activity in the waters around the still growing and now 45-foot whale had it excited and yet confused. It didn't know which to take first. It loomed well below the surface, listening, measuring, wondering what these shapes tasted like.

The biggest and loudest had passed it by once and the orca decided it needed another look as it started westbound, away from Picture Island. Like a bull, the orca cut through the water, pushing toward the surface and the giant fish made of steel with propellers instead of fins.

END

@severedpress
/severedpress

Check out other great

Cryptid Novels!

Hunter Shea

LOCH NESS REVENGE

Deep in the murky waters of Loch Ness, the creature known as Nessie has returned. Twins Natalie and Austin McQueen watched in horror as their parents were devoured by the world's most infamous lake monster. Two decades later, it's their turn to hunt the legend. But what lurks in the Loch is not what they expected. Nessie is devouring everything in and around the Loch, and it's not alone. Hell has come to the Scottish Highlands. In a fierce battle between man and monster, the world may never be the same. Praise for THEY RISE : "Outrageous, balls to the wall...made me yearn for 3D glasses and a tub of popcorn, extra butter!" – The Eyes of Madness "A fast-paced, gore-heavy splatter fest of sharksploitation." The Werd "A rocket paced horror story. I enjoyed the hell out of this book." Shotgun Logic Reviews

C.G. Mosley

BAKER COUNTY BIGFOOT CHRONICLE

Marie Bledsoe only wants her missing brother Kurt back. She'll stop at nothing to make it happen and, with the help of Kurt's friend Tony, along with Sheriff Ray Cochran, Marie embarks on a terrifying journey deep into the belly of the mysterious Walker Laboratory to find him. However, what she and her companions find lurking in the laboratory basement is beyond comprehension. There are cryptids from the forest being held captive there and something...else. Enjoy this suspenseful tale from the mind of C.G. Mosley, author of Wood Ape. Welcome back to Baker County, a place where monsters do lurk in the night!

Check out other great

Cryptid Novels!

J.H. Moncrieff

RETURN TO DYATLOV PASS

In 1959, nine Russian students set off on a skiing expedition in the Ural Mountains. Their mutilated bodies were discovered weeks later. Their bizarre and unexplained deaths are one of the most enduring true mysteries of our time. Nearly sixty years later, podcast host Nat McPherson ventures into the same mountains with her team, determined to finally solve the mystery of the Dyatlov Pass incident. Her plans are thwarted on the first night, when two trackers from her group are brutally slaughtered. The team's guide, a superstitious man from a neighboring village, blames the killings on yetis, but no one believes him. As members of Nat's team die one by one, she must figure out if there's a murderer in their midst—or something even worse—before history repeats itself and her group becomes another casualty of the infamous Dead Mountain.

Gerry Griffiths

CRYPTID ZOO

As a child, rare and unusual animals, especially cryptid creatures, always fascinated Carter Wilde. Now that he's an eccentric billionaire and runs the largest conglomerate of high-tech companies all over the world, he can finally achieve his wildest dream of building the most incredible theme park ever conceived on the planet... CRYPTID ZOO. Even though there have been apparent problems with the project, Wilde still decides to send some of his marketing employees and their families on a forced vacation to assess the theme park in preparation for Opening Day. Nick Wells and his family are some of those chosen and are about to embark on what will become the most terror-filled weekend of their lives—praying they survive. STEP RIGHT UP AND GET YOUR FREE PASS... TO CRYPTID ZOO

www.ingramcontent.com/pod-product-compliance
Lightning Source LLC
Chambersburg PA
CBHW072238190626
46809CB00018B/2836
9781922551306